NICKY DEUCE
Home for the Holidays

Also by Steven R. Schirripa & Charles Fleming

Nicky Deuce: Welcome to the Family

NICKY DEUCE

Home for the Holidays

STEVEN R. SCHIRRIPA & CHARLES FLEMING

Delacorte Press

Published by Delacorte Press
an imprint of Random House Children's Books
a division of Random House, Inc.
New York

www.randomhouse.com/kids
Educators and librarians, for a variety of teaching tools,
visit us at www.randomhouse.com/teachers

Library of Congress Cataloging-in-Publication Data
Schirripa, Steven R.
Nicky Deuce : home for the holidays / Steven R. Schirripa and Charles
Fleming. — 1st ed.
p.   cm.
Summary: Life in New Jersey seems boring to Nicky after spending the summer
in Brooklyn with his Italian-American family, so when his father invites
the relatives and Nicky's friend Tommy to their lavish home for a
New Year's Eve party, Nicky is sure that adventures will follow.
ISBN-10: 0-385-73258-9 (trade hardcover) — ISBN-10: 0-385-90276-X
(Gibraltar lib. bdg. hardcover)   ISBN-13: 978-0-385-73258-1 (trade
hardcover) — ISBN-13: 978-0-385-90276-2 (Gibraltar lib. bdg. hardcover)
1. Italian-Americans—Juvenile fiction.   [1. Italian-Americans—Fiction.
2. Family life—New Jersey—Fiction.   3. Bullies—Fiction.
4. Crime—Fiction.   5. Wealth—Fiction.   6. New Jersey—Fiction.]
I. Fleming, Charles.   II. Title.
PZ7.S34643Ne 2007
[Fic]—dc22
2006004584

The text of this book is set in 12.5-point Goudy.
Book design by Vikki Sheatsley
Printed in the United States of America
10   9   8   7   6   5   4   3   2   1
First Edition

To the loves of my life, Laura, Bria and Ciara
—S.S.

For Allison, Lesli, Sam, Nathan and Madeline
—and all Nicky's other young fans
—C.F.

NICKY DEUCE
Home for the Holidays

Chapter 1

The sky was gray. The trees were bare. Winter had come to Carrington.

Nicholas Borelli II, also known as Nicky Deuce, stared out at the dim afternoon as the smell of his mother's lentil soup rose through the house like a fog. It would be dinnertime soon.

Nicky sighed. Nothing interesting had happened that day. Nothing interesting would happen the next day. He closed his math book and went downstairs to eat.

Over dinner, his parents exchanged concerned looks.

"Nicholas, your mother and I have been talking," his father said. "You miss Brooklyn, don't you?"

Nicky said, "Kind of."

"You miss Grandma Tutti, and Uncle Frankie. And your friend Tommy?"

"Yeah. We had fun this summer," Nicky said.

His father nodded. "You're not having much fun now, are you?"

"I have fun," Nicky said. "Sometimes . . ."

"You haven't been to the skate park or the bike park in weeks," his mother said. "I haven't even seen you drawing."

It was true. He hadn't sketched anything in ages. Nothing seemed interesting enough to sketch.

"And you haven't been eating, ever since you came back from New York," his mother said. "Look! You've hardly touched your lentils!"

Nicky stared at the bowl of brown mush in front of him.

"So we've been thinking," his father said. "How about spending Christmas and New Year's with Grandma Tutti, and Uncle Frankie?"

Nicky beamed. "I get to go back to Brooklyn?"

"Better than that," his mother said. "They're coming to visit you!"

"Uncle Frankie and Grandma Tutti in *Carrington*?"

"And Tommy, too, if his mother says it's all right," Nicky's mother added. "Isn't that a good idea?"

A good idea? It was a *great* idea. Nicky said, "Yeah! Wow."

"We've got it all worked out," his father said. "Grandma Tutti and Uncle Frankie will come before Christmas. Tommy will come on Christmas, and all the guys from the old neighborhood will come right after that. We'll throw them all a giant party on New Year's Day."

"Wow," Nicky said again. "Which guys?"

"All of them!" his father said. "Jimmy, Oscar, Bobby, Charlie and Sallie."

"Maybe with his daughter, Donna," his mother added, and winked at his father.

"So," his father said, "what do you think?"

"Wow," Nicky said again, and dashed off to his room. "Yes!"

"Nicholas!" his mother called. "You haven't finished your lentils!"

Nicky flipped open his laptop and began IM'ing his pals.

chk it out, he typed. my dad's throwing a huge new yrs party. grandma tutti and my uncle frankie and my friend tommy from brooklyn are coming + all frankie's goomba friends. SO GOOD!

Three IMs came back right away. The first said, remind me, wuts a goomba?

Nicky sighed. There was going to be a lot of explaining to do.

The previous summer, Nicky had thought he was going to camp. But the sewage system there had blown up, so his parents had sent him to Brooklyn to stay with Grandma Tutti. He hadn't wanted to go. His grandmother was nice, but . . . *Brooklyn?*

Then he had gotten there, and so much had happened so fast that Nicky didn't even remember it all. Nicky and

Tommy had snuck into the movies, gone into business with a con man, and found themselves with a bootleg copy of *BlackPlanet Two*—the hottest computer game in the world—months before it was in stores. Then they'd been kidnapped by gangsters. Just when it had looked like they were doomed, Uncle Frankie had busted in and saved the day. An incredible adventure—all true.

The entire time, Nicky had thought his uncle was a gangster. Uncle Frankie kept weird hours and hung out with guys with names like "Jimmy the Iceman," "Oscar the Undertaker," "Charlie Cement" and "Sallie the Butcher." People on the street treated Frankie with respect, like he was a Mafia godfather or something.

It had turned out he was an undercover police detective. He'd rescued Nicky and Tommy and put the kidnappers in jail.

In other words, it had been the greatest summer of Nicky's life. Everything since had seemed dull and boring.

Until now. Suddenly Christmas and New Year's in Carrington looked pretty exciting.

For the next three weeks, the Borelli household was alive with activity. Day and night, delivery trucks and repair vans went up and down their quiet tree-lined street, past the rolling lawns and curving drives, past the elegant old Cape Cods with their rooftop observation decks, and the newer brick and stone colonials with their four-car garages.

Nicky's parents were busy preparing for the holiday season. His father arranged to rent a nearby bed-and-breakfast for his pals and their families. His mother arranged to have the living room painted. His father hired a caterer and a valet parking service. His mother hired a florist and had invitations printed.

As the holiday neared, Mr. Borelli's driver, Clarence, helped by picking up and dropping off packages of wine and liquor and party decorations. He spent an entire weekend hanging Christmas lights on the front of the house.

Clarence even spent an afternoon taking Nicky to do his Christmas shopping, first at the shops on Main Street and then at the mall by the interstate. Nicky was a good shopper. He had his own debit card and knew what he wanted. He bought a new terry cloth robe for his mother. He bought a black cashmere scarf for Grandma Tutti. For his father he got a tracksuit, sort of like the ones Uncle Frankie's goomba pals wore in Brooklyn. He bought Tommy a Super Phat Trux skateboard.

When Clarence went to get the car, Nicky sneaked back into the mall and bought a pair of leather driving gloves he'd seen Clarence admiring while they'd bought his father's tracksuit. Nicky put the gloves in the bottom of the skateboard bag so that Clarence wouldn't see them.

Most of the other holiday preparations went on without him. He was busy with his schoolwork—or he was supposed to be. Every time he said, "Can I help?" his mother answered, "After you finish your schoolwork." But he never finished his schoolwork. There was always another chapter of English to read, or another math problem to do, or another science test to prepare for.

Because his parents had been kind enough to buy him a PSP, an Xbox 360 and an iPod, Nicky felt obliged to spend a certain amount of time each day using those things. Some days there just wasn't any time left to finish studying.

Besides, he had to keep up with his friends. With IM'ing and talking on the telephone and posting on his MySpace page, Nicky kept busy. One night, he scanned a drawing of Grandma Tutti and a newspaper article about Uncle Frankie and posted them to three of his friends. Within an hour, he had IMs from Chad and Jordan—kewl, dude, i like cops, Jordan wrote—and a phone call from his friend Noah.

"Your uncle looks like a gangster," Noah said.

"I know," Nicky told him. "That's what I thought he was. He had guns in his room, and he had these friends with names like 'Sallie the Butcher' and 'Oscar the Undertaker.' I thought he was, like, the Godfather."

"Is he the one that gave you the gangster nickname—Nicky Deuce?"

"Yeah, that was his idea."

"But Tommy was the real tough guy, though—right? He's the one who saved you from that gang—when they were going to beat you to a pulp?"

"That's kind of exaggerating," Nicky said. "They were just—"

"He's the one who taught you how to stand up to Dirk Van Allen," Noah said. "That's all I need to know."

Dirk Van Allen! The very name made Nicky's heart thud a little more heavily in his chest. Dirk Van Allen! The biggest bully in Carrington.

Nicky had known Dirk since they were little kids, and Nicky had been scared of him since preschool. Dirk was big and strong—bigger and stronger than Nicky, anyway—and he was mean, too. He'd push a kid down and take his lunch. He'd push a kid down and take his ball. He'd push a kid down just for the fun of it.

In first grade, Dirk had knocked Nicky off the monkey bars. In third grade, Dirk had balled up his fists and said, "Dare you to fight, chicken."

"You are a noxious Neanderthal," Nicky had said—for he had just learned those new vocabulary words.

It stopped the bully in his tracks. "Neanderthal, eh?" he said. "What's that?"

For a long time after that, Nicky could slow Dirk down, or stop him altogether, by insulting him with unusual words. "You are a malingering miscreant," he said once. "You are a belligerent baboon."

But even Dirk Van Allen couldn't be fooled forever. In fifth grade, during a field trip from Carrington to the Museum of Modern Art in Manhattan, Dirk and a friend wanted the bus seat Nicky was sharing with Noah.

Dirk said, "Out."

Nicky said, "Dirk, you are a simpering—"

Dirk didn't wait for the rest. He grabbed Nicky in a

headlock and said, "Out, Borelli, *now*. Or I'll tear your head off."

That was the last time Nicky had tangled with him, until that winter. Nicky was sitting in the cafeteria watching Dirk and one of his friends bully Walter Wager out of his lunch money. Walter was a chubby kid, bigger than Dirk or his friend, but he looked scared.

Nicky put his head down on his table and thought, *If Tommy was here, he'd straighten them out.*

He imagined Tommy rescuing Walter, the same way he'd rescued Nicky on the first day of school in Brooklyn. He'd grab Dirk by the scruff of his neck and say, "Hey, you. Pick on someone your own size." Dirk would quiver with fear. He'd say, "We don't want any trouble here." And Tommy would say, "Well, you *got* trouble—with me. Buzz off before I brain you."

Dirk would slink away in shame. Tommy would be a hero. And Nicky, the boy who'd brought him to Carrington, would be a hero, too. Dirk's victims would all gather around. Three cheers for Nicky Deuce! Three cheers for Nicky Deuce!

"Wake up, princess."

Nicky jerked his head up. Dirk and his sidekick were standing over him.

Like all the Carrington boys, they wore gray slacks, white shirts, blue sports coats and blue ties. Dirk wore his like a wannabe rapper—tie hanging loose, shirttail out, pants hanging low.

"We're collecting donations for my favorite charity," Dirk said. "*Me*. So cough it up."

Nicky had a dollar in his pocket. Was saving a dollar worth getting roughed up? Or was making Dirk go away worth a dollar?

He tried to think of what Tommy would do. He tried to remember what Tommy had told him to do about the bullies in Brooklyn.

He couldn't. He reached into his pocket. "This is all I have."

"One crummy buck—from a spoiled rich kid like *you*?" Dirk said.

Nicky was a spoiled rich kid? Dirk's father was one of the richest, most powerful men in Carrington—treasurer of the Carrington Country Club, chairman of the Carrington Chamber of Commerce. Being called spoiled by Dirk Van Allen? That made Nicky mad.

He stood up, snatched the money out of Dirk's hand and said, "Forget about the dollar, Dirk, and buzz off."

Dirk looked stunned. No one talked back to Dirk Van Allen. He said, "Buzz off? Or else what?"

"I'll get Walter and all the other kids you've extorted money from to march down to the principal's office and make a report."

"Yeah, right," Dirk said, but he started moving away. "Next time I see you, you'd better have more money for me. *Nerd*."

Walter Wager had told the story to all Nicky's friends.

Noah had called him that night and said, "I heard about you and Van Allen today. Pretty cool."

"It wasn't any big deal," Nicky said.

"I want you to teach me what you said to him."

"All I said was 'buzz off,' " Nicky said.

"Well, it was *how* you said it," Noah replied. "That's what I want to learn. I want those tough-guy lessons you had in Brooklyn."

"My friend Tommy is coming to visit," Nicky said. "You can get your tough-guy lessons from him."

Chapter
2

The holiday preparations were almost complete. Nicky's mother had put new towels and soaps in the guest bathrooms. The gardener had planted poinsettias in the flower beds. Nicky and Clarence had picked out two beautiful Christmas trees—a huge one for the front yard, and a smaller one for the living room. Nicky and his mother spent an afternoon and an evening decorating them with bulbs, ornaments and tinsel.

"I haven't been this excited about Christmas since I was a little girl," his mother said.

"Me neither," Nicky answered, and they both laughed.

Even Nicky's father was jolly. He even came home early enough to join his family for dinner one evening.

"My six o'clock was canceled," he said, then loosened

his necktie and sat with them in the breakfast room, "which is too bad. I have my Fairport presentation tonight."

"What's the Fairport presentation?" Nicky asked.

"Low-income housing," his father said. "I'm going to turn the old Fairport brewery building into artists' studios and condos for the poor. It's going to be beautiful."

"You're going to be a slumlord," Nicky's mother said.

"No—I'm going to be a candidate for mayor. If the presentation goes well and Van Allen agrees to the financing, it's a done deal."

"Okay, Mr. Mayor," Nicky's mother said. "Go clean up, and I'll serve you some dinner."

"Great!" he said, then whispered to Nicky, "What's for dinner?"

"Tofu stroganoff," Nicky whispered back, because his mother was a vegetarian.

"Ouch!" his father said. "Isn't it great your grandmother will be here soon? She'll probably do some real Italian cooking. I could really go for a bowl of her pasta fazool!"

"This is just as delicious," Nicky's mother said, and lay a plate in front of his father. "And *much* better for you."

"I bet," Nicky's father said, pushing around a chunk of tofu with his fork. "I heard from Frankie today. He got Bobby Car Service to line up limos to bring all the guys and their wives up here. I've got the bed-and-breakfast in Newton all booked. Everything is in order."

"And is what's-his-name the butcher bringing his daughter?" Nicky's mother asked.

"Sallie the Butcher," Nicky's father said. "And yes, he is bringing his daughter."

That night, alone in his room, Nicky looked at the sketches he had made of Donna in Brooklyn. She had dark, wavy hair, and dark, shiny eyes. In every sketch she was smiling or laughing. Nicky got a funny feeling in his stomach when he thought about her. So he stopped thinking about her. He shut his sketchbook and checked to see who was online. Then he got an IM from Chad.

skool's over tomorrow. yay. I'm so done.

final quiz. u ready?

not, Chad answered. u?

not. let's study.

For the next half hour, the two boys passed questions back and forth.

who was charlemagne?

what's the magna carta?

how long was the hundred years' war—*psych!*

Then Chad wrote, i'm tired. r u going to the snow ball?

The Snow Ball. That was Carrington Prep's annual holiday party. Students from Carrington's sister school—Maple Hill Academy for Girls—came to Carrington for a semiformal night of dinner and dance at the Carrington Country Club. It was always held on the first Sunday of the new year, and it was always a very big deal.

For the grown-ups of Carrington, it was a chance to show off their town and their country club and their cars and their clothes.

For the young men of Carrington Prep, it was a chance

to pretend they were old enough to date. In preparation, they were taught how to dance a box step and a waltz, how to present a corsage, how to wear a necktie and how not to eat with their fingers.

i guess so. u?

boring. but yeah.

maybe i'll bring my friend tommy from brooklyn, Nicky answered. that'll shake things up a little.

The next day in school, Nicky aced the history quiz and put his name down for three tickets to the Snow Ball—for him, Tommy and Donna. The idea of them all together, in Carrington, almost made him dizzy. This was going to be some holiday!

Grandma Tutti arrived late that afternoon. Clarence had driven down to Brooklyn that morning, intending to return to Carrington in time for lunch. Grandma Tutti had had other ideas.

"We need to go to the store before we leave," she told Clarence when he knocked at the door of her Bath Avenue apartment.

"That's fine, Mrs. Borelli," Clarence said. "Is this your only bag?"

"That and what we get from the store," Grandma Tutti said. "Drive up to Eighteenth Avenue."

They left Brooklyn nine stores, five grocery bags and two and a half hours later. Clarence double-parked the large black Navigator while Grandma Tutti stopped at the pork store, the *salumeria*, the cheese store, the bakery, two delis, the butcher, a supermarket and the drugstore. The only place she didn't buy anything was the drugstore; she just went in to say goodbye to a friend. From the other shops, she bought parmesan cheese, mozzarella cheese, pecorino Romano cheese, pork sausages, steaks, loaves of bread, a thing like a baloney that she called *sopressata,* canned tomatoes, canned tomato sauce, dried pasta, garlic, herbs and a whole chicken.

"You know, Mrs. Borelli," Clarence said as he was loading the groceries into the car, "we have many of these items in Carrington."

"Not for nothing, Charlton, but I don't buy food from strangers," she answered. "Now we can drive."

Nicky's mother was waiting for them in front of the house when they arrived. She gave Grandma Tutti a big hug and said, "Thank goodness you're here. I was worried."

"I had to pick up a few things," Grandma Tutti said. "Charlie helped me."

Clarence was unloading grocery bags from the car. Nicholas' mother looked at them and laughed. "What's all this?"

"It's food," Grandma Tutti said.

"We have food here in Carrington," Nicky's mother said. "We even have food right here in the house."

"I know—but it's vegetarian," Grandma Tutti said, smoothing her black skirt and tugging at her black sweater. "This is *Italian* food, from the neighborhood."

"We have Italian food here, too," Nicky's mother said.

"I'll take you shopping. They have . . . meat, and pork, and chicken. All those things."

"Okay—as long as I don't have to cook with it, or serve it to my family," Grandma Tutti said. "My Frankie has a delicate stomach."

"I've seen Frankie's stomach," Nicky's mother said. "It doesn't look that delicate to me."

"He's a big boy, my Frankie," Grandma Tutti said. "Now if I could just get Nicky to eat right—and his father. Nothing personal, but they could both use a decent meal."

Nothing personal! Nicky's mother felt hurt. She blushed and put her hand over her mouth, then said, "Let's get these bags inside."

Nicky came home from school that afternoon to the heavenly smell of meatballs. He shouted, "She's here!" then ran to the kitchen. Grandma Tutti was standing over a saucepan, stirring with a wooden spoon.

"Nicky!" she called.

"Grandma!" he answered, and threw himself into her arms. Her clothes smelled like Bath Avenue. For an instant, he was back in Brooklyn.

"Put on your playclothes and help me cook," she said.

"What are you cooking?"

"Your favorite—what do you think?" Grandma Tutti said. "Meatballs in marinara sauce, with linguini, and a roast chicken, and roast peppers."

"Wow!" Nicky said. "Mom let you cook all that?"

"Do you think she could stop me?"

"It smells so good! I'll go change."

His mother was usually in the breakfast room when he got home, reading recipes, talking on the telephone or having coffee with one of her friends. That day she'd given the kitchen to Grandma Tutti.

Nicky went to the study. His mother wasn't there. He went past the living room and the dining room, to the library. She wasn't there, either. Nicky went back across the large empty house, walked upstairs and threw his backpack onto his bed. Then he went to the sewing room, and the laundry room. Nobody. He called out, "Mom!" Nothing.

When he was little, the big house had scared him. The study and the library downstairs were dark, grown-up places where the bad guys hid out. Until he was ten he couldn't stand to be downstairs alone at night. If he had to go down there, to get something from the kitchen or the breakfast room, he took a flashlight and ran the whole way. He'd often wished he had a brother or sister to go with him, so he wouldn't be scared. He'd often wished he had a brother or sister *period*—so he wouldn't be lonely.

But Grandma Tutti was there. And Tommy was coming! He wouldn't be lonely anymore.

He found his mother in the den, a cordless telephone pressed to her ear. The shades were drawn and the room was dark. Nicky heard his mother say, ". . . absolutely critical that no one in this house know that we're—" Then she saw Nicky and put the phone to her chest.

"Nicholas! How long have you been standing there?"

"I just walked in."

"It's not polite to eavesdrop, you know."

"Uh, yeah—I know," Nicky said. "I just wanted to tell you I was home."

"And?"

"And nothing. I'm gonna help Grandma Tutti with dinner."

"I'm sure she'll appreciate that. She's cooking *meat*. Now, if you'll excuse me?"

Nicky left the room, thinking, *Okay, that was weird. Is she bugged that Grandma Tutti is cooking food with meat in it? And who is she talking to like that, all secret, in the dark?*

In the kitchen, Grandma Tutti said, "You're going to do the roast peppers. You can start by telling me everything that's happened since the summer."

Nicky took a deep breath. "Well, school started, and then . . ."

At dinner that night, Nicky's father pushed back from his plate and said to Nicky's mother, "No offense, Elizabeth, but that's the best meal I've eaten in ages."

"Well, it's certainly the *biggest* meal you've eaten in ages," she said.

Nicky's father laughed. "I guess if you grow up eating the stuff, you never lose the taste for it."

"I'm glad you like it," Grandma Tutti said. "I don't like not having anybody to cook for. It's lonely."

"Don't you have friends you could invite for dinner?" Nicky's mother asked.

"What friends?" Tutti said. "Most of my friends are old like me, and they live with their children. They have their own families to cook for. The ones who are alone, like me—there's something wrong with them. Like my neighbor Mr. Moretti. He *should* be alone."

"Is he the gentleman who lives downstairs from you?" Nicky's mother asked.

"Gentleman—ha!" Grandma Tutti said. "If he wasn't a friend of my late husband's, he'd be out on the street! He's a drunken old bum."

"Speaking of bums who live in your neighborhood," Nicky's father said, "how's Frankie?"

Grandma Tutti smiled. "Frankie's fine. He's working hard, too hard, like always. He goes in and out, night and day, crazy hours. Sometimes he's on a job for three, four days at a time, and he can't even shave or shower. He comes home smelling like an animal."

"He *is* an animal—no offense," Nicky's father said. "He never did anything the easy way his whole life. Isn't he almost old enough to retire?"

"Two more years, he'll have his twenty," Grandma Tutti said. "Then he can start doing something else."

"When will he be here?" Nicky asked.

"On the twenty-third," his father said. "Just in time for Christmas."

"We'll all be together," Grandma Tutti said. "We can go to Mass. So I need to find out where's the church."

"Sure, Ma," Nicky's father said. "But what church?"

"Who knows?" Grandma Tutti said. "But you don't think

I'm gonna stay out here in the woods with no church, do you? I'll go where you go."

"Uh, great," Nicky's father said. "I'll make the arrangements with Clarence. Would you like to go this Sunday?"

"I'd like to go *now*," Grandma Tutti said. "Or don't you have Friday-night mass in the country? Not that you'd go on a Friday."

Nicky's father said, "I'll talk to Clarence now."

An hour later, in the backseat of the big Navigator, Tutti felt a little more at ease. *At least they* have *a church*, she thought, staring out the window as the countryside went by. *All these trees! No buildings! Where are all the people?* It was no wonder her Nicky had seemed lost when she had taken him to St. Peter's, in Bensonhurst. Who could even find another Catholic out there in the woods?

"Hey, Charlie!" she called into the front seat. "If you see one of those markets my daughter-in-law was talking about, you'll stop—right? I might buy a sausage or something."

"Yes, ma'am," Clarence said. "You bet I will."

Tutti sat back in her seat. Maybe being in Carrington was going to be okay after all.

Chapter
3

Within days the Borelli household was transformed. Grandma Tutti attended services at St. Monica's. She found an Italian deli that sold meats and cheeses and bread. Every morning Clarence drove her to church and took her shopping. Every afternoon she entertained guests while she cooked dinner or baked fresh bread or cakes and pastries.

Sometimes the guests were friends she'd made at church or at the deli. One afternoon three very old Italian ladies came for cookies and coffee. The next afternoon Grandma Tutti made cannoli for Father David, the young priest from St. Monica's.

Sometimes the guests were Nicky's mother's friends. Mrs. Feingold and Mrs. Carpenter, two of his mother's golf pals from the country club, stopped by one afternoon to meet Grandma Tutti—as if they were going to see some exotic animal at the zoo. The next afternoon two of her friends from the Carrington Prep PTA dropped by.

Tutti charmed them all. She told stories about her childhood, about Bath Avenue, about her late husband. She shared recipes and cooking tips and gave advice. Father David had a bad back; she told him to spread Vicks VapoRub on it and then lie down on a hot, damp towel. Mrs. Carpenter had sinus infections; Grandma Tutti told her to go to church every day and light a candle. Marian Galloway, Nicky's mother's best friend, who lived in the large Cape Cod next door, was recently widowed and dating again; Grandma Tutti told her, "I'm sorry for your loss. Learn to cook and you will find a new husband." She invited Marian to come around the following afternoon and watch her cook baked ziti.

Nicky's friends came around more often, too. Noah and Chad both asked if they could stay for dinner. They'd eaten Nicky's mother's cooking plenty of times. They liked Grandma Tutti's better.

Even Nicky's father was home for dinner most nights. He was still busy with his law practice, and with his plans to turn the old Fairport brewery building into housing for the poor—with Peter Van Allen's help.

But there was a problem. The Fairport deal had to be done by the first day of the new year. Van Allen said he might have trouble raising enough money by then. "I *have* the money, of course," he said. "But it's tied up in other projects." Nicky's father was going to have to invest some of his own money to finish the deal by January 1.

"Isn't that risky?" Nicky's mother asked. "I thought we weren't investing any of our money."

"I know," Nicky's father said. "But it's Peter Van Allen. It's not like we're going into business with some crook. It couldn't be safer."

But despite the difficulties, he managed to finish his work and get to the table almost every night in time for Grandma Tutti's braciole, or her steak *pizzaiola*, or her chicken parm.

Some nights, he'd find Nicky or his wife or both up to their elbows in red sauce as they helped Grandma Tutti put the finishing touches on the evening meal. Sometimes Marian Galloway would come, too. She and Nicky's mother would have a glass of wine and watch Grandma Tutti bake bread, make ricotta cheesecake or stuff a chicken with bread crumbs.

After dinner, Nicky's father would ask Clarence to build a fire. The four Borellis would sit in the living room—a room that, until then, had been used only for entertaining company—and just talk. Nicky's father found a CD compilation called *Christmas for Italians*. Every night for the next two days, they sat in front of the fire and listened to Frank Sinatra, Dean Martin and Tony Bennett sing "Silver Bells," "Winter Wonderland" and "Let It Snow! Let It Snow! Let It Snow!"

Then, just days before Christmas, it *did* snow. Nicky

went downstairs early one morning to find that Carrington *was* a winter wonderland. He whooped and hollered and made his mother bust out his snow gear. With his parka, ski pants and heavy boots on, Nicky went out into his backyard and spent the next two hours making a snowman and throwing snowballs at it. Then he turned on the jets in the hot tub, put on his bathing suit and timed how long it took to melt a snowball in hot water.

After lunch, Nicky had Clarence drive him and his friends Chad and Jordan to Glen Forks, a woody park where the boys sometimes went for a hike or a picnic.

That day, it was filled with kids on sleds, flying down the hiking trails, crashing into trees or each other, laughing and red cheeked with the cold and the excitement.

"Let's try going down the big hill," Nicky said, but no one would. "Come on!" he begged. "Halfway?" No one would. *When Tommy gets here*, he thought, *I bet he'll do it with me.*

Nicky and his friends spent the rest of the day carving trails in the snow and seeing who could go the farthest or the fastest or the longest time standing up.

Nicky went home exhausted. He couldn't *wait* for Tommy to come.

Uncle Frankie arrived, full of noise and packages and hugs, two days before Christmas. He sat with the Borellis in front of the fire that night, Grandma Tutti at his side, Nicky smiling up at him, Nicky's father and mother laughing at his stories. Nicky's father poured glasses of sweet dessert wine for Nicky's mother and Frankie.

"Look at this," Frankie said. "Fancy wine. A fire in the fireplace. Snow all around. It's like Christmas in the Sears catalog or something. Almost like a real family, *Amerigan* style!"

"I'm glad you're here," Nicky's father said. "I hate to think of all the Christmases you weren't."

"Ah, it's water under the bridge," Frankie said. "Let's let bygones be bygones. Hey, what's a bygone? Nicky?"

"I'm not sure. Something that's gone by already?"

"So, old acquaintance should be forgot, right? No, that's New Year's Eve."

"I think so," Nicky said.

"Whatever. I'm at home with my brother and his family, and it's the holidays," Frankie said, and raised his glass. "*Salute!* To your health!"

Nicky's father and mother raised their wineglasses. Grandma Tutti said, "If only your father was here!" and took out her handkerchief.

"Are you kidding? He'd run for his life back to Brooklyn!" Frankie said. "Can you imagine the old man here in Caramel Town?"

"He'd hate it," Nicky's father said. "All these trees! All this snow! Where's he gonna get a *Racing Form*? Where's he gonna buy his vino? Who's gonna get him some grappa?"

"He'd be proud of you, though," Frankie said. "This is some house. He'd want to know how many families you got living here. How many square feet is it?"

25

"Just over five thousand," Nicky's father said.

"Is that the house or the lot?"

"That's the house."

"Jeez," Frankie said. "I don't think I've ever been in a place this big. Except professionally. You remember that wiseguy Eddie Beets? He was a boss with the Marinello organization. He had a house on Long Island. We found bags and bags of heroin in the walls of his study. I said, 'Hey, Eddie, what's this?' He said, 'It looks like insulation. Ask the contractor.'"

"Well, I paid for mine the old-fashioned way," Nicky's father said. "I earned it, working my fingers to the bone like our old man did."

"Please! You're a lawyer," Frankie said. "And a very good one, I guess. I'm proud to be your little brother."

"Listen to that," Grandma Tutti said. "Isn't that nice? If only your father—"

"Look what I did," Frankie said. "She's going again. Stop, Ma!"

Grandma Tutti had been getting ready for days. The following morning, she began cooking the traditional Christmas Eve meal—the Feast of the Seven Fishes.

Before sunrise she was in the kitchen, cutting, chopping, cleaning, boiling, frying, steaming and roasting her way through a mountain of groceries. Nicky and his mother spent almost the whole day helping.

On the menu were seven kinds of fish, made into seven different traditional Italian dishes. There would be shrimp *oreganata*, fried calamari, linguine with clams, baked mussels, lobster Diavolo and more.

On the guest list were half a dozen of the Borellis' closest friends, including their next-door neighbor Marian Galloway, her daughter Amy, Tutti's new friend Father David—and Peter Van Allen and his wife, Gloria. The Van Allens were not friends, exactly, and Nicky certainly wasn't looking forward to seeing their son, Dirk. But Nicky's father needed Mr. Van Allen's money for the old Fairport brewery building. Inviting them seemed like a good way to butter him up. There wasn't a person alive who could resist Grandma Tutti's cooking. That and a few glasses of holiday wine, and Mr. Van Allen would be putty in Nicky's father's hands.

Clarence had built a huge fire in the living room. A catering service had sent over two waiters—dressed in matching black and white outfits, with festive red vests—to serve drinks and appetizers and help with dinner. Nicky's mother had decorated the house with wreaths and mistletoe and candles.

The guests stood in the living room with cocktails, listening politely while Father David more or less repeated Sunday's sermon. Then Uncle Frankie came into the room and everything changed. He shook hands with everybody, greeting them as if they were old friends. He said to Peter Van Allen, who had arrived with his wife but without his son, "Hey, Petey, how you doin'?" He slapped Father David on the back and said, "Hiya, Father. How's things with the Big Guy? I'm only kidding!"

27

Amy clinked glasses with Nicky and they sipped their eggnog. "Merry Christmas, Nicholas," she said, and flipped her blond hair. "I like your uncle. He's funny."

"He's great," Nicky said, then whispered, "How come Dirk's not here? Is he grounded or something?"

"Yeah, right," Amy said. "Like he's ever been grounded for *anything*. I think he had tickets to a hockey game."

That's a relief, Nicky wanted to say—but didn't. He didn't know the details, but he'd heard that Amy and Dirk were sort of boyfriend-girlfriend. He couldn't imagine how a nice girl like Amy . . . But it was none of his business.

When it was time for dinner, Nicky was disappointed to find he was seated far away from his uncle Frankie, and far away from Amy, too. He wasn't sure it was an accident. Amy was seated next to Mrs. Van Allen, which made sense—that boyfriend-girlfriend thing must be true—and Frankie was seated next to Marian Galloway. They seemed to be getting along well. *Very* well. Nicky's mother saw him looking at them, and she winked as if they were sharing a secret.

Dinner was served. Grandma Tutti had cooked a meal fit for royalty. One dish after another came from the kitchen, until the guests were filled to bursting.

"What a meal!" said Marian Galloway.

"Almost sinful!" said Father David.

"It's the most amazing dinner I have ever been served in a private home," said Peter Van Allen. "Borelli, I gotta hand it to you—and to you, Elizabeth."

"Thank you, but I take no credit," Nicky's mother said. "It's all my mother-in-law. She's the chef!"

"Three cheers for your mother-in-law, then," Mr. Van Allen said. "Here's to you, Tutti!"

Everyone at the table raised a glass. Grandma Tutti was, suddenly, silent. She looked into her plate.

"And three cheers for you, Borelli," Mr. Van Allen continued. "Thank you for inviting us here on this special occasion."

"Oh, it's nothing," Nicky's father said. "We're just flattered to have you join us tonight at our humble table."

Across the table, Nicky cringed. His uncle Frankie saw him. As the dishes were being cleared away and Nicky's father was moving the guests to the den, Uncle Frankie took Nicky's arm and said, "Take it easy, kid. Your old man's just doing what he needs to do."

"I know," Nicky said. "I've just never seen him act like that before. He doesn't bow down to *anybody*."

"I know," Frankie said. "But this is business."

When all the guests had said their thank-yous and gone home, and the two people helping in the kitchen had been paid and sent away, Nicky's mother and father started turning off lights downstairs.

"What are you doing?" Grandma Tutti said. "Where's everybody going?"

"Well, to bed," Nicky's father said. "We don't stay up all night like you city people. It's almost eleven o'clock!"

"But what about mass?" Grandma Tutti asked.

"What about mass *what*?" Nicky's father asked back.

"Father David is coming to pick us up."

"Are you kidding?" Nicky's father asked. "At this hour?"

"Of course at this hour," Grandma Tutti said. "It's for midnight mass! Have you forgotten everything? Are you telling me that no one in your house goes to midnight mass on Christmas Eve?"

"Uh, yes," Nicky's father answered. "I guess I am telling you that."

"Okay, Mr. Big Shot from the suburbs," Grandma Tutti said. "You're too old for me to boss around. And too old for me to teach. But Nicky isn't. Maybe you don't have the old traditions. I *do*. And someone has to observe them with me. I'm taking Nicky to midnight mass."

Nicky's father found him getting into his pajamas.

"Hold it, Nicky," he said. "Your grandmother is going to midnight mass. She says—no, she *insists*—that she's taking you with her. If you really don't want to go, I won't let her. But if you don't mind . . ."

"I get it," Nicky said. "I don't mind. It might be kinda fun."

"Uh, yeah," his father said. "Sure."

"Do I have to wear a sports coat?"

"Yes, and a tie. I'll help you."

Thirty minutes later Nicky and his grandmother were cruising along the darkened Carrington streets, headed for St. Monica's. Nicky, bundled up tightly in an overcoat and scarf and wearing gloves, felt cozy and warm in the

30

backseat. When they arrived, he didn't want to get out and go into the cold cathedral.

But it was warm and cozy in there, too. The lights were low. A million candles had been lit. Organ music was coming from somewhere far away. Father David led Nicky and his grandmother to a pew near the front and said, "We'll sit here. I have to go say hello to a few people."

Nicky settled into his seat next to Grandma Tutti. Then he fell asleep.

Chapter
4

The next morning it was Christmas. More snow had fallen in the night. The backyard, from Nicky's bedroom window, was a perfect blanket of white. He raced downstairs to find the Christmas tree surrounded with presents, and Grandma Tutti drinking coffee in the kitchen. He gave her a giant hug.

"Merry Christmas!" he whispered, as he knew his parents were still sleeping.

"Merry Christmas!" she whispered back. "Why are you whispering?"

"I don't want to wake up Mom and Dad."

"In this big house!" Tutti said. "You could beat on pots and pans and no one would hear. Help me finish my coffee cake, and then come open a present I bought you. . . ."

Nicky spent the morning opening presents—new shoes for lacrosse, a book of American short stories, a new set of charcoals for drawing and, from Clarence, a paisley necktie.

"For that Snow Ball thing of yours," Clarence said. "So you look sharp."

Nicky's parents were now standing near the tree smiling as he opened his last present from them. It looked like a CD. Nicky was, honestly, not too excited about that one. His parents had good taste in music and all. It just wasn't *his* taste. As he picked it up and pulled at the paper, his mother said, "Now, your father and I weren't sure you'd really *like* this present, but we hope it's okay."

When Nicky saw the logo—a huge dark sun—he said, "*BlackPlanet Two?*" Then he shouted. "No way!"

"Oh yes wa-ay," his mother said, laughing.

"After what happened this summer," his father said, "we weren't sure you'd still be interested in this."

"Are you kidding?" Nicky said. "It's the best!" He leapt to his feet and gave each of his parents a hug.

It was almost as good watching everyone else open the presents Nicky had bought for them. Uncle Frankie loved the overcoat Nicky and his mother had picked out for him. Grandma Tutti loved the cashmere scarf and said she would wear it to church every day.

Uncle Frankie laughed when he saw the tracksuit Nicky had bought for his father. "He's gonna turn you back into a goomba," Frankie said. "Which you might need, if you're gonna stay in business with guys like Van Allen."

"Why?" Nicky's father asked. He looked hurt. "What's wrong with him?"

"Nothin'," Frankie said. "I just got a funny feeling from him. Does he know I'm a cop?"

"He knows you're an undercover detective," Nicky's dad said. "I told him. He was impressed."

"That's okay, then," Frankie said. "It just makes some guys nervous."

Nicky's mother modeled the new robe and said it was beautiful. And Clarence was delighted by the driving gloves. "You must've seen me looking at these, Nicholas," he said. "That's a very considerate present."

But the biggest present of all came in the late afternoon. Nicky was reading by the fire when the phone rang. A minute later, his mother came into the room and said, "That was your friend Tommy. He's down at the train station. Clarence is pulling the car around. Would you like to go with him?"

"Yes!" Nicky said.

Tommy was waiting on the platform, standing with his hands in his pockets and a battered book bag slung over his shoulder. He looked small and cold and lost. Nicky ran up to him, shouting, "Tommy!" and skidded to a stop. Tommy smiled, and stuck his hand out.

"Hey, pal."

"Hey."

"So, I made it."

"Yeah."

"Pretty cold, huh?"

"Very."

"So, you live around here?"

"About five miles away. Where's your stuff?"

"This is my stuff," Tommy said, and showed Nicky his book bag.

"Uh, great," Nicky said. "Let's go."

Tommy stared out the window as Clarence drove them home. He seemed amazed by everything he saw.

He pointed at a huge wooden mansion poised atop a rolling hill. "What's that?"

"That's the country club."

He pointed at a set of stately stone buildings surrounded by graceful trees hung with snow. "That another country club?"

"That's Carrington Prep—my school," Nicky said.

"It looks like Buckingham Palace or something."

"It's just a school," Nicky said. "But up here to the left is the skate park. And over there—well, down that road a little way—is the mall where they have indoor laser tag. And the movie theater. We'll go there."

"Sounds good."

"And this is my street."

Clarence had left the main road and was driving down a tree-lined street fronted by broad, sloping lawns, white with snow and watched over by stands of pine, maple and oak trees.

Clarence pulled into the Borellis' driveway and stopped the Navigator in front of the garage. He got out and went around to open the door to the house.

Sitting in the car, Tommy said, "You gotta be kidding."

Nicky said, "What?"

"This is your *house*?"

"Why not?"

"It looks like a—I don't know—castle or something. You really live here? I mean, just *you*?"

"Well, there're some rooms over the garage where Clarence hangs out during the day."

"So he lives here, too?"

"No," Nicky said. "He has his own apartment. That's just for him to hang out during the week if he's not driving."

"So the house is basically just for you and your folks?"

Nicky laughed. "Come in and see."

Tommy stared at everything and was almost completely silent. He barely said hello to Nicky's parents. He smiled at Nicky's grandmother but grimaced when she gave him a hug.

"You look starving," she said when she turned him loose. "And you feel like a bag of bones. Let me make you some macaroni."

"That's okay," Tommy said. "I'm not really hungry."

"Come upstairs," Nicky said. "I'll show you your room."

Going across the house, Tommy said, "This is nuts."

"What?"

"Look at this place!" he said. "I mean, not for nothing,

36

but what's all this for? You could set up a bowling alley in here. Check this out."

Tommy paced off the living room, walking the length of it and then the width. "You could put my whole house in this room and still have room left over. Unbelievable."

Upstairs, Nicky said, "This is your room. Here's your bathroom. There's towels and stuff."

Tommy looked out the window and said, "Who lives next door? Donald Trump?"

"No. That's my friend Amy's house. You'll like her."

"Yeah? She's pretty?"

Nicky had never thought of Amy that way, but he said, "Actually, yes. But she's just my friend—like, since I was a little kid."

"Uh-huh. And where do you sleep?"

"My room's just down the hall. Here."

Tommy looked in and whistled. "You got that *BlackPlanet* poster."

"I got the new *BlackPlanet Two*, too," Nicky said.

"You're kidding—the one we coulda ripped off this summer?"

"Yes, but this time it's legal. It was a Christmas present from my parents. What did you get from yours?"

"Nothing," Tommy said. "Nothing yet, anyway. My mom said my presents would be waiting for me when I got back. Between you and me, I think she's going shopping at those after-Christmas sales."

"Oh," Nicky said. "So maybe that means more stuff, since it'll be cheaper, right?"

"Something like that," Tommy said.

"Well, I got you something for *now*," Nicky said. "Come on."

Nicky led Tommy back downstairs, to the Christmas tree, where only two packages remained. Nicky handed Tommy the first one and said, "Open this. It's from me."

Tommy tore the paper off, then pulled the box apart. "A skateboard? Whoa!" he said. "But . . . I don't know how to ride a skateboard."

"I'm going to teach you to skate like Tony Hawk," Nicky said. "When I'm done, you'll be the skateboard king of Brooklyn. Now open the other present."

Tommy quickly unwrapped the smaller package.

"No way," he said.

"Way," Nicky said.

"Unbelievable," Tommy said. "Is this one legal, too?"

"Of course," Nicky said. "Now we can play *BlackPlanet Two* online after you go home."

Tommy hung his head. "It's too much," he said. "And you know what I got for you? Nothing."

"*Fugheddaboudit*," Nicky said, and laughed. "You came to visit me! That's the best Christmas present of all."

Frankie and Nicky's father had a drink while the two boys were getting reacquainted. Nick poured two glasses of whiskey and sat with Frankie in the library.

"To your health," he said.

"*Salute*, as we say in the old country," Frankie said. "So, tell me about this Van Allen guy."

"Cheers," Nicky's father said. "What do you want to know?"

"Well, how come he's such a big deal?" Frankie asked. "Is he one of those guys who arrived on the *Mayflower* with the silver spoons in their mouths?"

"I don't think so. I think he's just rich."

"That's it?" Frankie said. "That's all it takes to get elected King of Carrington?"

"You have to be rich, and you have to be smart—and he's both. He moved here when the real estate market was just starting to get hot, and he made some smart investments, and he made a fortune. He got interested in some local charities, and he made some big friends by making some very big donations. Next thing you know, he's on the board of this and the board of that."

"And how'd you meet him?" Frankie asked.

"You couldn't miss him," Nicky's father said. "He was everywhere—every fund-raiser, every charity event, every party. He's very ambitious."

"You two should get along, then," Frankie said. "Elizabeth told me about your plans for Fairport—Mr. Mayor."

Nicky's father blushed. "Cut it out, Frank. I got involved with Fairport because it's the right thing to do. Nice apartments for poor people and artists. Plus it looks good for my law firm. All that other talk, about me running for office, that's just a lot of talk. If it happens, however, that the people of Fairport want me to represent them . . ."

Frankie clapped Nicky's father on the back. "Congressman Borelli! Senator Borelli! A Borelli in the White House! Good for you, Nick. The old man would be proud."

"Don't jinx it," Nicky's father said. "The paperwork is being done now. First business day of the new year, it's ours."

"What a great way to celebrate the new year," Frankie said.

"Just keep your fingers crossed for me. After all the sweat I've put into it, I'd hate for anything to go wrong now."

Tommy had trouble falling asleep that night. He wasn't used to sleeping in a strange bed. He wasn't used to being out of Brooklyn. It was so . . . *quiet* here. No cars. No car horns. No car alarms. No sirens. It was creepy. Maybe you got used to it after a while.

He couldn't stop thinking about Nicky's giving him such a nice present, and his giving Nicky nothing at all. He couldn't stop thinking about telling Nicky that his mom hadn't given him anything, either. He tried to remember the look on Nicky's face. Had he been surprised? Had he been laughing? Did he think Tommy had a bad mother?

He hadn't seen any of that in Nicky's face. Nicky had just smiled and said, "Fugheddaboudit."

He was a good guy, Nicky. And a good friend. Thinking that made Tommy feel even more ashamed of himself, though. *You should get your good friend a good Christmas present*, he thought. *If you had any money, that is*.

The next morning, Nicky got Tommy dressed in snow clothes and had Clarence drive them to Glen Forks. Clarence had loaded the Navigator with sleds. Nicky's mother had made sandwiches and filled a thermos with her own homemade vegetable soup. Grandma Tutti had filled a basket with her own homemade cookies. Clarence dropped the boys and their picnic basket at Glen Forks before driving on to Nicky's father's office.

Nicky took Tommy to his favorite run, a short steep hill that ended in a long flat area. Nicky said, "You can lie down on the sled on this one, and drag your foot for the brakes. Take it easy the first time down, so you see how fast it is, okay?"

Tommy nodded.

"Do you want me to go down first?"

"What for?" Tommy said, and threw himself down the hill.

Tommy was a speed demon. Soon he was showing Nicky new tricks to do with a sled.

"Watch this," Tommy said, and began building a kind of ramp. On his next run down the hill, he shot up the ramp and sailed into the air, then crashed half buried in a snowbank.

He emerged, grinning, and said, "You gotta try this!"

Nicky and Tommy sledded until they were exhausted. After a lunch break, Nicky said, "Let's build a snowman."

They made his eyes and mouth out of small stones, his nose from a crooked stick, and his hair from a crown of leaves. Nicky said, "He looks a little like—"

"Look out!"

Too late. A flying snowball caught Nicky in the back of the head.

"Quack, quack!" a voice called out. "Nice duck, Borelli!"

It was Dirk Van Allen, with three of his rowdy pals.

"These guys are asking for a beating," Tommy said, and began to walk toward Dirk.

"No," Nicky said, "it's just a snowball fight. Come on! We'll cream them."

"Then look out!"

Too late! Nicky got hit again, in the chest that time.

Tommy scooped up a handful of snow and formed a snowball. He cocked his arm and threw—*bam!* His first snowball caught one of Dirk's friends square in the ear. The boy looked shocked, then angry. He scooped up a snowball.

It was war. Nicky and Tommy hid behind their snowman, who soon lost his nose and his crown of leaves. Tommy took one hit to the chest, but he landed quite a few on the enemy. Then he prepared a giant snowball and said, "Watch this. Big Bertha. Bombs away."

He cocked his arm just as Dirk hurled a snowball that flew like a rocket. It cracked into Tommy's chin and knocked him to the ground. Nicky grabbed a handful of snow and prepared a counterattack. Tommy didn't get up. Nicky said, "Come on! They're charging us!" but Tommy didn't answer. Nicky dropped his snowball and fell to his knees. There was red all over the snow. At Tommy's side was a sharp stone that Dirk had buried inside his last snowball.

Nicky reached inside his jacket for his cell phone and quickly dialed. "Clarence! We need you back here now!"

It took an hour in the emergency room and four stitches to close the gash on Tommy's chin. By the time they got home, it was late afternoon. The light was going. Tommy was wrapped in gauze. The doctors had given him a shot, so he sounded fuzzy when he talked. Nicky's mother put him straight to bed.

Then she marched Nicky to the kitchen and said, "I've got to call Tommy's mother and explain what happened. What in the world were you doing throwing rocks?"

Nicky said, "We weren't. We were throwing snowballs. Then Dirk Van Allen buried a rock in a snowball and hit Tommy in the face."

"It must have been an accident," his mother said. "I can't imagine Peter Van Allen's son doing something like that on purpose."

"Give me a break, Mom," Nicky said. "He's the biggest bully at C.P. He always does stuff like this."

"We'll discuss this when your father gets home," she said. "In the meantime, I'll need his mother's telephone number."

Nicky was happy to learn that Tommy's mother hadn't answered the phone. He'd been afraid she'd insist on Tommy coming home right away. But when Nicky's mother had called, there had been nothing.

"Isn't that strange?" she asked. "There wasn't even an answering machine."

"I think they're kind of poor, Mom," Nicky said.

"Too poor for an answering machine?" she replied. "Ridiculous!"

Nicky's father wasn't happy with the story when he got home that night. "That's a dirty trick," he said over dinner. "I'll talk to his father."

"You should do more than that," Uncle Frankie said. "Somebody ought to teach that kid a lesson."

"That little boy needs a smack in the head," Grandma Tutti said, and waved her wooden spoon.

"Well, I assume his father, after I speak with him, will discipline him for throwing rocks at other children," Nicky's father said.

Frankie looked at Nicky, who shrugged.

"Yeah, right," Frankie said. "His dad won't do nothing. This isn't the first time he's done something like this, right, Nicky?"

"He's been like this since preschool."

"He's a bully," Frankie said. "So he's a coward. All bullies are cowards. They're afraid of everybody, so they make themselves feel strong by finding someone who's afraid of *them*."

"Listen to Sigmoid Freud," Grandma Tutti said.

"I'm just saying," Frankie said. "Until that kid gets a wake-up call, he's not gonna stop beating on Nicky."

"Well, he's not going to get a wake-up call from my son, or from you," Nicky's mother told Frankie.

"Like I said, I'll talk to his father," Nicky's father said. "I'll get it straightened out."

Nicky wondered if he would. He knew he and Tommy were in the right, and Dirk Van Allen was in the wrong. But he remembered the way his father had kissed up to Mr. Van Allen at the dinner party. Like Frankie said, it was business.

The next morning, Tommy's jaw was sore and his chin was bruised, but he wanted to go to the skate park just the same.

"I'm fine, Mrs. Borelli," he said.

"I don't know," Nicky's mother said.

"He doesn't eat like he's sick," Grandma Tutti said. "Five pieces of bacon! Plus pancakes."

"I'll keep an eye on him, Mom," Nicky said. "Can't we just go for an hour?"

"As long as you both wear gloves and the wrist guards.

And the helmets. And stay warm. And speak to your mother."

"Yes!" Nicky said. "I'll ask Clarence if he can drive us."

"And you try your mother again now," Nicky's mother said.

There was no answer at the Caporelli home. Nicky said, "Is that weird?"

"No," Tommy said. "No one ever answers the phone there. It could be a bill collector or something. So, can we go, or what?"

The skate park was mostly covered, so the ramps and half-pipes were clear of snow. Nicky started Tommy out on the flats and gradually moved him to the slopes. Tommy was a natural skater. Within an hour, he was riding like a pro.

"You should take it easy," Nicky said. "Doesn't your chin hurt?"

Tommy reached up and poked his bandage. "I forgot about it."

"Well, you wouldn't want to fall on it, right?"

"Who's gonna fall?" Tommy said, and shot down a ramp.

Around three o'clock the boys bumped into two of Dirk Van Allen's friends—the ones who had stood by and watched Dirk pelt Tommy with the rock.

"Nice bandage," one of them said. "Did you fall off your board?"

"Very funny," Tommy said. "Come over here and I'll give *you* something to put a bandage on, too."

"Forget it, garlic breath," the boy said. "We don't play with pepperonis like you."

The two boys skated away. Tommy started after them. Nicky grabbed his arm.

"Forget it, Tommy," he said.

"Forget it? Did you hear what they called me?" Tommy said. "Back home, guys get killed for saying stuff like that."

"Down here, they get laughed at—or just ignored," Nicky said. "Let's do the half-pipes again."

Grandma Tutti was cooking when the boys got home that afternoon. Marian Galloway was there, along with Mrs. Feingold and Mrs. Carpenter. Grandma Tutti was rolling out pasta dough and cutting wide strips of lasagna when Nicky and Tommy went into the kitchen for a glass of juice.

"How wide should the noodles be?" Mrs. Feingold asked. "One inch? Two inches?"

"Inches!" Grandma Tutti laughed. "Who needs inches? You make it just wide enough like this. But not too wide!"

"And how long do you cook the noodles?" Mrs. Carpenter asked.

"Until they're done," Grandma Tutti said. "But don't overcook them."

"More wine, Doris?" Marian Galloway said.

Upstairs, Tommy said, "I don't think those friends of your mother's are going to learn very much."

"They should just be quiet and watch," Nicky said.

"That's what I did, and I already know how to cook all kinds of things."

"You like that? Cooking?"

"Sure," Nicky said. "Why not? I like *eating*."

"I guess," Tommy said. "Not for nothing, but it's kind of girly."

"Says who?" Nicky said. "Almost all the famous chefs are guys. Like, uh, like Molto Mario, and . . . Chef Boyardee!"

"You're weird."

"Yeah, I know," Nicky said. "Listen, it's probably better if we don't say anything about those guys at the skate park today, you know? I don't want to get my uncle Frankie riled up."

"I understand," Tommy said. "If he heard that kid called me garlic breath, it'd be all over, wouldn't it?"

"*Fugheddaboudit*," Nicky said, and laughed.

That night, after dinner, Nicky and Tommy sat roasting marshmallows and making s'mores.

"This is great," Tommy said. "I've never been camping before. This is what you do at Camp Whatchamacallit?"

"Camp Runnamucka. For that, you sleep in a tent and get bitten by bugs. And you do rowing, and canoeing, and hiking, and archery, and . . ."

"It sounds like the L.L.Bean Olympics," Tommy said. "This is better."

"Yeah, this is pretty good." Nicky speared another marshmallow. "Also, there are these two parties coming up. One of them is the Snow Ball. It's a big deal in Carrington.

48

Dinner and dancing. Kind of formal, but kind of fun. Everyone brings a date. That's next Sunday night. And tomorrow night there's a party at my next-door neighbor's house. Wanna come with me?"

"Why not?" Tommy said. "So far, life in Carrington is pretty sweet."

Chapter
5

Early the following morning, Uncle Frankie came into Nicky's room and said, "Come on, kid. We're going down the shore."

"Now?" Nicky wiped sleep from his eyes. "But isn't it snowing?"

"We're going to check out this joint your father has lined up," Frankie said. "You wanna come with us?"

"Let me wake up Tommy," Nicky said. "We'll come downstairs."

Over breakfast, Frankie said, "Hey, Tommy. How's that chin?"

Tommy pushed gently on the bandage. "Not so bad," he said.

Frankie laughed. "I should see the other guy, right?"

"Yeah, if Nicky had let me have a piece of him."

"What a tough guy," Frankie said. "So where is this place?"

"It's in Newton," Nicky's father said. "Right on the sand, by the boardwalk. For the summer, you have to reserve a year in advance. In the winter, it's empty. So I rented the whole place."

Nicky's father drove, with Frankie in the passenger seat and the boys in back. They took the interstate south, then a little highway through some marshy wetlands. Soon they were driving down a windswept beach road. Each beach town had its own boardwalk, lined with arcades, restaurants and snack bars selling hot dogs and hamburgers or fish-and-chips and ice cream. Everything was closed for the winter.

A hundred years before, the tiny town of Newton had been a weekend getaway for wealthy people. Stately homes stood over the dunes, looking out at the sea. One of them was now the Newton Manor B&B, an elegant three-story Victorian building that looked like a wedding cake.

"What's the 'B and B' part mean?" Frankie said. "Isn't it a hotel?"

"It means 'bed-and-breakfast,' " Nicky's father said. "It's like a hotel, except they serve you a big breakfast, and the rooms are more like bedrooms in a house. Sometimes you share a bathroom with someone down the hall."

"That's skeevy," Frankie said, looking disgusted. "What if you don't know the people?"

Nicky's dad shrugged.

"So that's why they gotta throw in the free breakfast," Frankie said. "B and B my eye. It should be called B.Y.O.B.—bring your own bathroom."

The owners were an elderly couple named Mary and Marvin Monroe. "We're looking forward to meeting your friends," Mary said. "I hope they'll be comfortable here."

"How many bathrooms you got?" Frankie said.

"Why, six," Mary said.

"And how many bedrooms?"

"Fourteen," Mary said.

"Oh boy," Frankie said.

"Nicholas, you and Tommy go check out the beach while we settle up here," Nicky's father said.

The boys stood on the dunes. The ocean was white-capped and rough.

Tommy said, "This sure ain't Coney Island, or Brighton Beach. This is like—the *beach*. Look at those waves."

"I'll race you to the water," Nicky said. "Don't get wet! Go!"

Chilled by the windy beach, the boys were just thawing out when they got back to the house for lunch.

Nicky said, "Mom, can we go for a swim after lunch?"

"Of course," she said. "But turn on the hot tub now, so it'll be ready after you eat."

Tommy looked at Nicky, and at Nicky's mom, and then laughed.

"Yeah, right," he said. "A swim! Some joke."

"Seriously," Nicky said. "Come on. You can help me turn the hot tub on. Get your jacket."

"You make sure Tommy doesn't get his bandage wet," Nicky's mother said. "The doctor said three days."

Nicky led Tommy out the back door, across the back deck and along a snowy path leading down a sloping lawn. At the bottom, covered with a heavy plastic shell, was a swimming pool with a rock-lined hot tub beside it. Nicky went into the pool house and pressed a button. The plastic shell began to draw back, revealing the steaming blue swimming pool. Nicky punched another button. The hot tub began to bubble.

"My mom keeps the pool warm 'cause she swims laps," Nicky said. "The Jacuzzi will be hot by the time we finish lunch."

Tommy stared at the water. "Swimming in the snow," he said. "Unbelievable."

After lunch, the two boys soaked in the hot tub and splashed in the pool. Tommy dared Nicky to jump out of the pool and make an angel in the snow. Nicky dared Tommy to do it first. They both ran screaming back to the hot tub and sank in to their chins.

Suddenly, there was a pretty blond girl standing by the pool, wrapped in a heavy parka and wearing a chilly smile.

She and Tommy stared at each other.

"Hi, Amy," Nicky said. "Wanna swim?"

"Oh *please*—no," Amy said. "I just came to see who

could possibly be making so much noise. It sounded hideous."

"Sorry about that," Nicky said. "It was me. This is my friend Tommy, from Brooklyn."

"Howya doin'?" Tommy said.

"Oh dear," Amy said. "Is he the one who taught you how to be a groompa?"

"*Goom-ba*," Nicky said. "Can I bring him to your party tonight?"

"Of course," Amy said. "Wear something . . . dry."

"Thanks for the tip," Nicky said.

"Bye-aye," Amy said, and turned away.

When she was gone, Tommy said, "So what's with the prom queen?"

"She's okay," Nicky said. "She was just trying to impress you."

"Well, it worked," Tommy said. "What a big stuck-up baby."

The first of the gang from Brooklyn arrived late that afternoon. Clarence went down to the train station in the Navigator and returned with Charlie Cement; Jimmy the Iceman and his girlfriend, Janice; and Sallie the Butcher, along with his new wife, Carol, and his daughter, Donna. Nicky and Tommy, locked in a *BlackPlanet Two* battle to the death, heard them arrive and went downstairs.

"Hey, Donna!" Tommy said. "Howya doin'?"

"Hi, Tommy," Donna said. "Hello, Nicky."

"Hi."

"You should see the place Nicky's dad rented for you guys," Tommy said. "It's right on the beach. It looks like a wedding cake. Fourteen bedrooms!"

"Is that how many you have here?" Donna asked, gazing around.

"No," Nicky said, feeling shy. "Not that many."

"Are you sure? This is the biggest house I've ever seen in my life."

"Not really," Nicky said. "Most of my friends' houses are way bigger than this."

"Some friends," Donna said. "It must be hard for you to make do with less than they have."

"Cut it out, you two," Tommy said. "I wish you were staying here. There's a pool! We went swimming this afternoon."

"Get out of here," Donna said.

"Swear," Tommy said. "It's heated!"

At dinner, Nicky said, "Mom, do you think Donna could stay here, instead of down in Newton? That way, she could come to Amy's party."

"Hmmm," his mother said. "She could sleep in the guest bedroom. Carol? What do you and Sal think about that?"

"Is she safe here with these hoodlum boys of yours?" Sal said. "I heard that Nicky Deuce is a regular Romeo."

Nicky blushed until his face was on fire.

His mother smiled. "I'm pretty sure she'll be okay," she said. "I'll keep an eye on her."

*　*　*

A wooden fence and a tiny stream, frozen in the snow and crossed by a short wooden footbridge, separated Nicky's house from Amy's. The three friends, bundled up and feeling good, set out across Nicky's backyard. Beyond the swimming pool at the bottom of the yard, Amy's house glimmered through the trees like a tower of light as they went through the gate into her backyard.

"It looks enchanted," Donna said. "How come you don't lock the gate?"

"Like anyone would come in and steal anything?" Tommy asked. "Everyone who lives around here already owns everything they need."

"You can joke," Nicky said. "But last year there was a string of burglaries. All the families got these electronic alarms. My dad said the real thief was the guy selling the security systems."

"Maybe he was the guy breaking into the houses, too," Tommy said. "Good way to drum up business."

"You're so cynical," Donna said.

"I am not," Tommy said. "What's 'cynical'?"

"It means— Look out," Nicky said. "Here come the Dobies."

A pair of sleek black and brown Dobermans dashed toward the three friends, moving fast and growling low. Tommy went pale and stood as still as a statue.

"It's okay," Nicky said. "They're nice."

Tommy was paralyzed. The dogs went to him first. He began to shake with fear.

"C'mere, Duke," Nicky said. "Atta boy. See? They're nice doggies."

Tommy was sweating. "Get 'em away from me."

"They're sweet," Donna said.

"Get 'em away!" Tommy said. "I'm telling you, I can't stand dogs."

The Dobermans lost interest and trotted off. Nicky said, "I'm sorry. I didn't know you were afraid of dogs."

"I'm not afraid of them," Tommy said, wiping his face with his sleeve, his voice shaky with fear. "I just don't like them, is all."

"Okay," Nicky said. "I'll keep them away from you."

They were greeted at Amy's front door by a pair of maids in black dresses and white aprons who took the children's jackets and mittens. The hallway rang with Christmas music.

The house was full of kids, all of whom Nicky knew well. Passing from the foyer, into the library, into the living room, into the den and taking a glass of eggnog and a piece of fruitcake, Nicky introduced Donna and Tommy to everyone they saw. They met his friends Jordan and Noah, who were sitting in the den playing a Game-Cube. They bumped into Chad, who was getting a glass of punch.

"This is Chad," Nicky said. "Chad, this is my friend Tommy, from Brooklyn."

"Oh, yeah? Howya doon?" Chad said, and put up his fists. "You wanna piece of me?"

Tommy stepped back. "I beg your pardon?"

"I said, do you want a piece of me?"

"Chad—what are you doing?" Nicky said.

Chad put his hands down and said, "I don't know. I was just doing a Brooklyn thing, you know. Like in the movies."

"O-kay," Nicky said. "We're going to get some punch."

Moving away, Tommy said, "What's that kid's problem?"

"Who knows?" Nicky said. "He's watching too much TV."

A crowd of girls was gathered by the punch bowl. Nicky introduced Tommy to his classmates Caroline, Christian, Kyra, Kendra, Keisha and Dakota.

"Okay, that's funny," Tommy said as they walked away. "In my neighborhood, it would be 'I'd like you to meet Pete. I'd like you to meet Mary.' That's it. No fancy names. Maybe one guy named Anthony, and one girl named Angela. What's with Kyra or Keisha, anyway? They sound like Japanese cars. 'Introducing the new Kendra—from Toyota!' "

"Louder, Tommy," Nicky said. "I don't think Kendra heard you. There's Amy."

She wasn't wearing her parka anymore but had changed into a pair of sleek black slacks and a gray cashmere sweater. She was the most elegant person Tommy had ever seen.

"Nicholas—and Tommy, right?" she said, and then smiled at Donna. "I'm Amy. Are you another of Nicholas' friends from Brooklyn?"

"This is Donna," Nicky said. "We met at summer

school. She and her family came up for my dad's New Year's party. They're staying in that spooky old bed-and-breakfast in Newton."

"Not really!" Amy said. "That place is haunted. I refused to go there when I was little. My aunt owned it and used it as her summer home."

"Your aunt lived in Newton?" Nicky asked.

"My aunt *was* a Newton," Amy said. "What did you do to your chin?"

Tommy's hand went to his bandage. He had forgotten. He said, "This? I had a snow, uh, accident. A snowboarding accident. In a snowmobile."

"What a bore," Amy said. "And don't you think my party is boring, too? Maybe if we got rid of this appalling music. Mother! Excuse me."

"What a bore!" Tommy mimicked. "Who is she—the Queen of England?"

"She's the Queen of Carrington," Nicky said. "But she's right about the music, anyway."

Then the music changed. The speakers went *thump thump thump*. Someone said, "Ah-ooo," and the young people began to dance, carefully.

Most of the kids were shy. They moved their feet and hands a little and mostly stood in place, swinging their elbows and pretending they were dancing.

Not Tommy. He moved, and he grooved. He rocked and rolled. Nicky had never seen anything like it, except on VH1. Tommy could *dance*.

Tommy started out dancing with Donna while Nicky

sort of danced near them. Then another girl came over and said, "Yeah!" and started dancing with Tommy. Then she said, "Cassandra! Come here!" After two songs, there were five or six girls all dancing together, with Tommy in the middle, while a handful of other dancers stood back and watched.

"Ladies! Please!" Tommy said after five or six songs, and pushed his way over to Nicky. "I need a Coke or something. I'm dyin' here."

"Wow!" Nicky said to him. "You can really dance!"

Tommy shrugged. "I do okay. But what's with the rest of you guys? Nobody else around here likes to dance?"

"Not like that," Nicky said. "They're all too shy."

"Too shy to dance? That's like being too shy to play baseball."

"Whatev," Nicky said. "Let's go find Donna."

Tommy grabbed a plate of cinnamon rolls as they went past the refreshment table. They found Donna dancing politely with Chad.

"Donna's a good dancer, huh?" Nicky said. "She deserves a better partner than that."

"The little tough guy! You want me to get rid of him?"

"No, he's okay," Nicky said. "But I was thinking. Maybe you could teach me later—"

"Hey, look!" a big voice said. "It's Frosty the Snowman."

Tommy turned around fast. Nicky didn't have to. He knew the voice belonged to Dirk Van Allen. Nicky turned slowly.

"Hey, Frosty!" Dirk said. "You hurt your chin?"

"That was a dirty trick, Dirk," Nicky said. "That was cheating."

"All's fair in war and battle," Dirk said. "Or don't you know your Shakespeare? Hey, Amy. I was just saying hello to your guests. Do you let *anybody* come to your party?"

"I guess so," Amy said. "You're here, for example."

"Oh, funny," Dirk said. "I was talking about Pizza Boy."

Tommy stepped forward and pushed Dirk hard in the chest. The bully rocked back on his heels and then sat down on the floor. As he struggled to his feet, his face beet red with rage, Tommy pushed him to the floor again.

"Stay down," he said. "Or I'll beat you down."

Dirk hesitated, looking around for help.

"Not so tough without your boys, huh?" Tommy said. "Well, I'm here with *my* guys. You watch your mouth or I'll throw you out of here. Got it?"

Dirk got to his feet slowly, without answering. He brushed off his pants, breathing hard, his face burning. He said, "You'll be sorry for this."

"Sure thing," Tommy said. "And merry Christmas to you, too."

Dirk left, slamming the big front door behind him so hard, the windows shook. Someone turned up the music. Amy drifted over to where Tommy, Nicky and Donna stood with their eggnogs.

"That was nice," Amy said.

"Dirk started it," Nicky said. "And Tommy didn't know that Dirk was your, uh, you know, boyfriend, or whatever."

"My *boyfriend?*" Amy said. "What are you talking about?"

"Well, that's what he says," Nicky said.

"He's hallucinating," Amy said. "I'm glad he's gone."

"Yeah?" Tommy grinned. "You liked how I took care of that?"

"I thought it was revolting," Amy said. "And I'd like you to leave. Now. Buh-bye."

Outside, bundling up in their jackets and mittens, the three friends walked across Amy's yard and into Nicky's, through the gate and across the frozen stream.

"I don't think they do things like that up here, Tommy," Donna said.

"Things like what?"

"Things like fighting."

"Well, excuse me," Tommy said. "The guy was bothering us. I pushed him down. He stopped bothering us. What's the problem?"

"You got us thrown out," Donna said.

"Yeah," Tommy agreed, then turned to Nicky. "No good?"

"I don't know," Nicky said. "You let Dirk know who was boss."

"Maybe so," Donna said. "But I don't think you impressed Amy much."

"Maybe she secretly thinks you're a hero," Nicky said.

"Maybe she secretly thinks I'm an idiot," Tommy said.

"Not secretly," Donna said.

"Thanks," Tommy said.

"Well, at least you got Dirk off our backs," Nicky said.

"For now," Tommy said. "But he's not done. We haven't seen the end of that guy."

Back at the house, Nicky's mother had set up the guest room for Donna and put a futon mattress on the floor, next to Nicky's bed, for Tommy.

"Look at this," Tommy said. "My fourth night in the country, and I get kicked out of my own bed."

"Quit whining," Donna said. "Sleepovers are fun. It's like camping."

"Yeah!" Nicky said. "Let's make some more s'mores."

"S'more s'mores," Tommy said. "Let's make *lots* more."

Downstairs, Nicky's mother said, "Tommy, don't you think you should call your mother?"

"I don't know," Tommy said. "What for?"

"To let her know you're okay," she said. "You can use the telephone in the library."

When she had gone, Tommy said, "Which one is the library?"

Nicky led him there. Tommy looked at his watch.

"This is stupid," he said. "My mom and Harvey will be krunked by now, if they're home. And Gramps will be asleep."

Nicky thought about that for a moment, then said, "What do you mean, 'krunked'?"

"I mean, it's nine o'clock," Tommy said. "She'll be drunk."

Nicky remembered sitting in Tommy's apartment with him. He remembered Tommy's mom, and his gramps. He understood.

"Well, you don't *have* to call now, if you don't think it's a good idea," Nicky said.

"It's not," Tommy said. "Let's don't and say we did."

"Let's don't and not say anything," Nicky said. "You can try again tomorrow."

"I'll try again tomorrow."

"So, s'mores?"

"S'mores."

Chapter
6

Sallie the Butcher was back at the Borelli house early the next morning to pick up his daughter and to tell Frankie and Nicky's father to come to Newton.

"We're playing poker," he said. "A marathon game. All day long. All the guys."

"Deal me in," Frankie said.

"Deal me out," Nicky's father said. "I've got to work."

"It's Christmas!" Sallie said. "It's New Year's!"

"I've got an important meeting. You guys go ahead. I'll try and come down later."

It was after ten-thirty when Tommy and Nicky went downstairs.

"You sleepyheads!" Grandma Tutti said. "You missed breakfast."

"No breakfast?" Tommy said. "I could eat a horse!"

"We don't got horse," Grandma Tutti said. "But I can make pancakes or waffles."

"Waffles!" Nicky and Tommy said at the same time.

"You help, then," she said. "Nicky, get the eggs. Tommy, get a big bowl from that cupboard."

Stuffed with hot food, the two boys were deep into a round of *BlackPlanet Two* when Nicky's father looked in on them an hour later.

"Can I have Clarence drop you guys somewhere?" he asked. "I've got this meeting in Newark."

"What's in Newark?" Nicky asked.

"The building commission," his father said. "I have to make my pitch to them, with Peter Van Allen. Wish us luck."

"Okay," Nicky said. "Can Clarence take us to the mall?"

"Or you could stay and have coffee with Grandma Tutti and Father David and the old ladies from St. Monica's."

"The mall, please."

"Take your cell phone, then," his father said. "Call Clarence when you're ready to come home."

The after-Christmas sales had started. The stores were humming with activity. But the food court was almost empty, and no one was in line at the movie theater. Nicky and Tommy bought lemonades in the food court and stood staring at the marquee.

"Kid stuff," Tommy said.

"Sequels," Nicky said.

"Let's check out the arcade," Tommy said.

"Okay," Nicky said. "But I'm warning you, it's lame."

The boys spent the next two hours playing old-fashioned pinball machines, taking breaks now and then to go back to the food court so Tommy could "steal" a refill on his lemonade. Tommy was very sneaky about it. He was having so much fun that Nicky didn't have the heart to tell him the food court offered unlimited free refills on all their drinks.

"We're killing these guys," Tommy said as he sipped his fourth refill. "But I gotta go to the bathroom."

"That's what you get," Nicky said. "They're down here."

On the way back, Tommy said, "Hey—there's your ma."

Nicky looked. Tommy was right. Nicky said, "Mom! Hey, Mom!"

Far down the mall, Nicky's mother seemed to stop and glance at the two boys. Next to her was a tall man with dark hair. Then Nicky's mother darted into a store.

Nicky said, "C'mon!" He and Tommy jogged down the mall.

But there was no sign of her.

Tommy said, "No way that wasn't her, right?"

"It sure *looked* like her."

"Who was the guy with her?"

"I don't know. But this is the art supply store where I get my paints and stuff."

"Let's go inside."

Nicky led Tommy down an aisle that had fat charcoals and big pads of sketch paper. The aisle, and the store, was empty. Nicky waved at the man behind the counter.

"Who's that?" Tommy asked.

"Mr. Silver," Nicky said. "He owns this place."

"Is that who your mom was with?"

"No."

"So who was it?"

"Someone she knows from one of her charities, I guess."

"Then what was she running away for? And where'd she go?"

"I don't know," Nicky said. "Maybe it wasn't her. But again, I walked into the living room the other day and she was whispering on the phone to someone, and she freaked out when she saw me."

"Wow," Tommy said. "You think she could be working on some scam or something?"

"Tommy—it's my mom."

"Then maybe she's got a boyfriend."

"Tommy! Shut up!"

"I don't know!" Tommy said. "Could it be some kind of weird vegetarian thing?"

"Like what?"

"I don't know," Tommy said. "I'm betting on the boyfriend scenario."

"No way!" Nicky said. "That's just crazy."

"Then, what?"

"I don't know," Nicky said. "But not *that*. Forget that. Don't say that again."

"Okay," Tommy said. "I'm sorry. You wanna try that other pinball machine now?"

"No," Nicky said. "Let's go home. I'll call Clarence."

She wasn't sure whether Nicky had seen her. It had been a close call, though. She was getting sloppy. Going to her car, she said, "We have to be more careful about this. Maybe you shouldn't park your car so close to the house. And you should call me first, too, to make sure he's not there."

"You don't think he knows?"

"I *know* he doesn't," she said. "And if he finds out— well, I don't know what I'll do. He *mustn't*. It would ruin everything."

Nicky reached Clarence in the car. He and Nicky's father were driving back from Newark and were not far from the mall. Clarence said, "We'll meet you out front in about fifteen minutes."

Nicky was quiet on the drive home. Tommy said, "We played pinball and drank lemonade."

"Well, I had a productive day, too," Nicky's father said. "Van Allen is along for the ride. The building commission gave us provisional permission to go forward."

"That sounds good," Tommy said, "if you're sure he's not a creep like his kid."

"No, I think he's okay," Nicky's father said. "Nicky's met him. Didn't you think he seemed like a good guy, Nick?"

"I guess," Nicky said.

"Thanks for the vote of confidence," his father said. "But you'll see."

Dinner was weird. Nicky couldn't look his mother in the eye. Grandma Tutti had cooked a feast, as usual—mozzarella marinara, chicken parmesan, broccoli with garlic—but Nicky had no appetite. Tommy watched his friend squirm. He tried to help.

"So what'd you do today, Mrs. Borelli?" he asked.

"Oh, this and that," Nicky's mother said, giving Tommy a careful look. "Errands, mostly. There's still so much to do for the big party."

"Really?" Tommy said. "Did you go shopping at the mall?"

"Not today, no," Nicky's mother said. "Although it feels like I practically *lived* there during Christmas."

"Really? 'Cause me and Nicky—ow!"

Tommy reached down and clutched his ankle. Nicky had just kicked him hard under the table.

"What in the world was that?" Nicky's mother said.

"I twisted my ankle at the skate park," Tommy said. "It's still bothering me a little."

"You should put ice," Grandma Tutti said. "After dinner, I'll make you an ice pack."

"Great, 'cause I think it's swollen—*now*," Tommy said.

After dinner, Tommy said, "What about another swim?"

"What about if you call your mom?"

"What about if you shut up and mind your own business?" Tommy said. "Anyway, it's too late."

"Okay," Nicky said. "In that case, we could . . . What about . . . What about if you teach me to, you know, uh . . ."

Tommy grinned. "After last night, right?"

Nicky said, "Yes. I just think I need some, like, moves."

Tommy grinned some more. "You *know* you do. You need to learn how to handle yourself."

"Exactly."

"You need to learn how to take care of business."

"Well . . ."

"You wanna feel like a *man*!" Tommy grinned. "All *right*. I promise you, in half an hour I can have you ready to go head to head with almost anybody—except me, of course."

"I don't have to be better than you—yet."

"Don't get ahead of yourself," Tommy said. "Where do you want to do this?"

"We can go in the library," Nicky said. "There's a CD player in there."

"Hey, there's nothing wrong with a little music."

In the library, Nicky said, "What should I put on?"

"Whatever you want," Tommy said. "It doesn't matter."

"Should it be something slow, or something with a beat?"

"Who cares?" Tommy said. "Whatever inspires you. 'Eye of the Tiger.' Or the theme song from *Rocky*."

"Not a dance song, like 'Macarena' or something?"

Tommy gave him a long look. "Why? Is the other guy Spanish or something?"

"I don't know," Nicky said. "What other guy?"

"Look, it doesn't matter," Tommy said. "C'mere. Watch me. The most important thing to start with is the footwork, okay? Stand there. Spread your feet out a little. Bend your knees a little, too. Now, get your hands up, about like so."

Nicky did what Tommy said. He stood facing him, feet apart, knees bent, hands at shoulder height.

"Now make a fist, but with your thumbs *outside* the fist, not inside, like this," Tommy said, and showed Nicky his fists.

"What's that for?" Nicky asked. "Why do you make a fist?"

"Very funny," Tommy said. "Now, start moving your feet a little, like this, right? Shift your shoulders. You're watching the other guy. You're waiting for him to move. You're getting ready."

"Should I start the music now?"

Tommy put his hands down. "What is it with you and the music? Do you think there's going to be an orchestra playing when this stuff goes down?"

"Isn't there?" Nicky was confused. "It just makes sense. Shouldn't you be listening to music when you learn to dance?"

"*Dance?*" Tommy stared at him.

"Well, yeah," Nicky said. "What did you think?"

"I thought you wanted me to teach you how to *fight*."

72

"No!" Nicky said. "I want to learn how to dance."

"Oh. All right," Tommy said, but he looked a little let down. "I can do that. Maybe later I can teach you how to fight, too."

Nicky got some CDs from his room and brought them down to the library. Tommy inspected them—"Too fast. Too depressing. Not bad."—and made his selections.

"We'll start with the easy stuff, okay?" he said. "Look at me. Stand here. Now, you feel the beat? Just pick up your feet a little and move your arms."

Nicky did, while Tommy watched.

"Oh boy," Tommy said. "This could take a while."

They practiced for an hour. Nicky began to feel like a dancer. Tommy showed him the simple stuff, then the more difficult stuff.

"You're doing great," Tommy said. "Remember, it takes most guys years to develop these moves."

"It took me a long time to learn the box step and the fox-trot," Nicky said. "I had to go to cotillion for, like, two years to learn that and the waltz and a bunch of other junk."

"I bet you could teach me pretty quick, though, huh?" Tommy said.

"Why would you want to know?"

"I don't know," Tommy said. "But it seems like, with a girl like Amy, you probably ought to know how to do the slow-dance stuff."

"A girl like Amy, eh?" Nicky said. "You little devil."

Tommy blushed. "I'm not saying anything."

"Well, I'll show you anyway—just in case," Nicky said. "Put on something slow."

"Yeah? Then?" Tommy said.

"Give me your hand," Nicky said. "Like this."

It felt a little weird. Nicky stood with his left hand raised, holding Tommy's right hand, and his other hand on Tommy's hip. But Tommy was a good student. Within minutes, he was going one-two-and-three-four like a pro.

"This ain't so hard," Tommy said.

"No, it's simple," Nicky said. "Now you try leading."

The boys switched positions. Tommy took Nicky's hand and began moving him around the floor, counting, "One, two, three, four . . . ," out loud.

The lesson was almost over when Clarence walked in, carrying one of Nicky's father's briefcases and fumbling in his pockets for his keys. He saw the two boys dancing and stopped suddenly. Nicky and Tommy broke apart.

"Sorry, guys!" Clarence said. "Didn't mean to barge in."

"No problem," Tommy said. "I was just teaching Nicky here how to, uh, fight."

"Really?" Clarence looked embarrassed. "It looked more like—well, whatever, right?"

"Well, actually," Nicky said. "We—"

"Hey—it's cool," Clarence said. "You guys are friends. Why shouldn't you dance together, right?"

"Uh, right," Nicky said. "But actually it was a dance *lesson*. I was teaching Tommy the box step and the waltz. He was teaching me some dance steps. Some of his *moves*."

"What moves were those?" Clarence asked. "You know all the latest steps or something?"

"I don't know," Tommy said. "I was just going like this."

Tommy did a quick turn. Clarence started laughing. "Smooth!" he said. "Can you do this?"

Clarence put down the briefcase and the keys and did a few steps.

Nicky laughed and said, "Clarence! That's great. Let me put on some music."

Tommy said, "Show me that again," and Clarence did.

For the next ten minutes, Clarence showed Tommy, and Tommy showed Clarence. Then Clarence said, "Now you, Nicholas."

Nicky clumsily did a few turns.

"*Very* smooth," Clarence said. "Now check this out."

With that, he did a wicked spin, went into the splits and hit the floor.

"Wow!" Nicky said. "Can you teach me that?"

"I don't know," Clarence said. "Let's try."

Going to bed that night, worn out from the dancing, Nicky was quiet. Tommy said, "You wanna do some quick *BP Two?*"

"No, thanks," Nicky said. "I think I'll just go to sleep."

"You tired from all that dancing?"

"A little."

"You still freaked out about your mom?" Tommy said.

"A little."

"It's probably nothing," Tommy said. "If you knew what was going on, it'd probably be something really normal."

"Yeah?" Nicky said. "Like what?"

Tommy thought for a minute. "Okay, it's not normal. But I bet it's nothing bad."

"Bad?" Nicky said. "Like what?"

"I don't know," Tommy said. "But it's your *mom*. She's not like other moms."

Nicky raised himself up on one elbow and looked at Tommy. "What do you mean?"

"I mean, she's Mrs. Borelli," Tommy said. "She's your mom. She's, like, the best mom. Bringing me up here, that was her idea, right?"

"Yeah."

"Well, there you go. She's the best, right?"

"Yeah."

"Besides that, you gotta remember, even if she's your mom, she's still a girl. Right?"

"So?"

"So girls are not like us, is all I'm saying," Tommy said. "It's worth remembering. Girls are not like us at *all*."

Nicky woke up early the next morning. It was only seven-thirty. He got up anyway.

He found Grandma Tutti making coffee downstairs and gave her a hug.

"Good boy," she said. "Now you can help me make breakfast. We're going to have *sfogliatella*. Nicky, bring me the flour."

Nicky helped his grandmother break the eggs, break the butter into little pieces and mix the dough. Grandma Tutti rolled it out onto the kitchen table, patted her hands with flour and showed Nicky how to cut it into little squares.

"Now we gotta make the filling," his grandmother said. "Get the ricotta."

Something outside the window caught Nicky's eye as he was going to the refrigerator. He said, "Is that Mom?"

"No," his grandmother said. "She's upstairs. Give me a sharp knife, please."

"Wait," Nicky said. "I saw Mom. What's she doing outside?"

Nicky went to the window. His mother was standing at the bottom of the garden, near the pool, with a man wearing black jeans and a black parka. He was nodding while Nicky's mother pointed at the ground and made a circle. Was it the same man he'd seen her with at the mall?

"Nicholas!" Grandma Tutti said. "Come away from that window. I need the knife before my dough gets too warm!"

Nicky pulled himself away. Whatever was going on, he wasn't supposed to see it. He decided to pretend that he *hadn't* seen it. Like Tommy had said, his mom might be his mom, but she was still a girl. Maybe he should ask Donna what she thought about it. She was a girl, too, and a smart one. But on the other hand, what if it was something weird, or bad? He wouldn't want Donna to know anything weird or bad about his family.

Nicky got the knife for his grandmother, who said, "Okay. Now we got to cut the dough in little lines, like so."

Tommy came downstairs an hour later, his hair sticking up and a big smile on his face. The house had filled with the smell of baking pastry. Walking into the kitchen, he said, "It smells like something good in here."

"*Sfogliatella*," Nicky said.

"Bless you," Tommy said. "What's for breakfast?"

More snow had fallen in the night. The backyard looked like a painting. Clarence came in, stamping his feet and clapping his mittened hands together.

"Cold!" he said. "*Crazy* cold! Is your dad ready yet?"

"I haven't seen him," Nicky said. "Why are your knees all wet?"

"I had to put snow chains on the car," Clarence said. "The roads haven't been plowed, and your father has a meeting."

"About the thing with Mr. Van Allen?"

"I don't know," Clarence said. "Maybe."

"Have some coffee," Grandma Tutti said. "And you can try the first *sfogliatella*. Nicky, get Charlton a plate."

"It's Clar— Thank you, Mrs. Borelli. These look delicious."

"Look nothing," Grandma Tutti said. "How do they taste?"

Clarence bit into one and sighed. "Perfect."

When Nicky's father came downstairs, he said, "You boys got big plans for the day?"

"Not really," Nicky said. "Not with this snow, and the roads messed up."

"It's pretty bad out there," his father said. "I was just

listening to the news. The interstate is shut down. Do you want to come see my building? Better than being cooped up here."

"Sure, Dad," Nicky said. "Tommy?"

"Yeah," Tommy said. "Can we take some pastries?"

"It's *sfogliatella*," Grandma Tutti said. "You can take two each."

The little town of Carrington was half-asleep in the fresh snow. Most of the shops were closed. The streets were empty. Everything was muffled and silent. Clarence drove the Navigator slowly, its tires making a soft crunchy sound on the pavement.

The old brewery building was in a broken-down section of Fairport, New Jersey, a city that had once been a big commercial fishing port and had later become a factory town. Now it was a collection of abandoned brick buildings and a little downtown strip that was being taken over by what Nicky's father called yuppies.

"Look at this," Nicky's father said. "Around the corner, on First Street, there's a bookstore, a sushi bar and an Internet café. You can get a cappuccino and a California roll, but there's no police station, no public telephones that work and no post office."

"Is that bad?" Nicky said.

"Yeah—but it's beautiful!" his father said. "It's a great opportunity. We're really getting in on the ground floor. Stop here, Clarence. Look at my building. Isn't it great?"

It wasn't. It was old and dirty. The brick was chipped

and stained. The windows had no glass in them. Nicky's father was beaming.

"We're going to turn this into a real showplace. Clarence, drive over to First Street."

Nicky's father dropped the two boys on the main street and said, "We'll come back for you in an hour. You can cruise around, get a bite to eat, whatever you like. Just stay out of the abandoned buildings, including the stuff on the beach. All right?"

The boys spent half an hour wandering the waterfront. Across the sand was a ruined amusement park, where a roller coaster now crumbled into the sea. Closed storefronts along the empty boardwalk still had signs for a tattoo parlor, a pinball arcade, a hot dog stand, a fun house and a doughnut shop.

"That reminds me," Nicky said. "We gotta get my grandma to make *zeppoli*."

"She *makes* those? The doughnut things?"

"Yeah."

"Oh, man. I love *zeppolis*. They sell them at Santo Pietro. You remember—the school festival."

"I remember the school festival, but I don't remember the *zeppoli*," Nicky said.

"That's because you were too busy thinking about Donna."

Nicky blushed.

"See? Ha!" Tommy said. "You *still* got a crush on her!"

"Cut it out."

"Cut *you* out," Tommy said. "I could use a *zeppoli* right now. It's freezing, and I'm hungry again."

"Let's go in the café," Nicky said. "I bet they got something."

The boys sat in a high-backed wooden booth and ordered hot chocolate and cannoli.

"Not as good as Grandma Tutti's," Nicky said, "but not bad."

"Delicious," Tommy said with his mouth full. "I was starving."

"We'll get something good for lunch, I bet," Nicky said. "I think Grandma Tutti is going to make lasagna."

"Let's go back outside and look at that amusement park thing."

"I don't know," Nicky said. "My dad—"

"Relax," Tommy said. "We won't do anything stupid."

There was a fence around the old ticket booths, but someone had cut through it and left a gaping hole leading down to the old midway. Nicky and Tommy slipped inside and walked among the buildings. Hand-painted signs, faded almost to white, promised a sideshow with a bearded lady, an India rubber man and someone called Sealo the Seal Boy. Next door to that was a haunted mansion. Next to that was a house of mirrors.

At the end of the row of ruined buildings was an old Ferris wheel, creaky and rusted. Tommy climbed into the lowest cart, then climbed up to the next one. The metal groaned when he stepped onto it.

"Come on," Tommy said, and put his hand down to drag Nicky inside. "Look at the view. I bet you could see Manhattan if it was clear."

"And not so cold," Nicky said.

"I wish we had another hot chocolate," Tommy said. "Whoa—get down."

The boys got low in the Ferris wheel carriage. Nicky whispered, "What?"

"Don't look now, but three guys just walked through the fence, and they're coming this way."

"Oh, great," Nicky said. "Is it my dad?"

"No," Tommy said. "It's a man in a suit and two wiseguys."

Nicky peered over the edge of the carriage. "It's Peter Van Allen," he said. "The father of the kid who hit you with the snowball."

"What's he doing here?"

"He's supposed to be my dad's partner on the brewery building."

The three men came closer. Nicky and Tommy scrunched down low. The footsteps stopped just beneath them.

"What a place," a heavy voice said. "When I was a kid, this was paradise."

"And look at it now," another voice said. "Destroyed."

"We're going to change all that—me and my 'partner.'"

The three men laughed. Nicky raised his eyes at Tommy. He whispered, "That's Van Allen talking."

The men moved a few feet away. Nicky strained to hear what was being said.

"What's the deal with this Borelli guy anyway?" the heavy voice said. "You know I hate doing business with Italians."

"He's not Italian—not like you mean," Van Allen said. "He's just a lawyer. But he's the guy who's making this deal look legal."

The three men laughed again.

"He's got big plans—first the brewery building, then the old cannery, then the old city hall," Van Allen said. "There's a fortune for us here. So once we get the building permits, he's out."

"Just like the old days, Patty," the other voice said.

"Don't call me that," Van Allen said. "*Ever*. The old days are gone, and Patrick Arlen is dead and buried. Don't go digging him up now—or the next guy I kill and bury will be *you*."

"Don't worry—*Peter*," the heavy voice said. "Soon as the deal closes, we'll take care of Borelli. We'll make him an offer he can't refuse."

The three men moved away, their footsteps heading back toward the amusement park gates. Nicky and Tommy stayed low. When a minute had passed, they heard a car door slam and an engine start. They peeked out in time to see a black town car pull away from the boardwalk.

"Wow," Tommy said. "That was intense."

"Yeah," Nicky said. "I gotta warn my dad."

"I don't think so," Tommy said. "We'll get a licking because we went into the amusement park. Which he said don't."

"You're right," Nicky said. "He'll be mad. I'll get grounded. Or he'll take away the *BP Two*."

"He'd do that?"

"Or worse," Nicky said. "When he says don't, he means *don't*."

"Then what are we gonna do?"

"I don't know," Nicky said. "I have to think."

That night, lying in his bed, Nicky felt scared. His father was in business with a crook who was going to double-cross him. His mother was doing something she had to hide from him—and maybe from his father, too.

Nicky had to do something but had no idea where to begin.

Chapter
7

The following day was filled with preparations for the big Borelli bash. The catering company delivered food. The liquor store delivered wine. The musicians came and set up their instruments in the living room. Nicky's mother spent hours dashing from room to room, issuing orders through the telephone.

"We're going to need more ice."

"I need those cakes delivered by noon."

"Where are those flower arrangements?"

Then the party rental company came with the tables and chairs, and the tent for the backyard, and the heaters that would keep it warm. Within an hour, the backyard was transformed into a party room.

Grandma Tutti was busy in the kitchen, and she had

company. In addition to Nicky's mother, Mrs. Feingold and Mrs. Carpenter were back, plus two other women Nicky recognized but hadn't really met.

"Hello," Nicky said. "Good morning, Grandma."

"Good morning, Nicky!" his grandmother said, and gave him a kiss. "These are my students!"

"We're the first students for your grandmother's cooking school," Mrs. Feingold said. "Today, we're learning marinara sauce and homemade pasta!"

"And the best part?" Nicky's mother said. "It's a vegetarian pasta dish!"

"It's macaroni—or noodles," Grandma Tutti growled. "Pasta is a phony-baloney word made up by restaurants."

"It smells great," Nicky said, and sniffed a pot of sauce.

"I can't believe it's all so simple!" Mrs. Feingold said. "Olive oil, garlic, tomatoes and a little basil? Who knew!"

"And a pinch of sugar, right?" Nicky asked.

"Out!" his grandmother said, and pushed Nicky away from the stove. When he was out the door, she whispered, "You'll tell them all my secrets!"

"They don't know about the sugar?"

"Shhh!" Tutti hissed. "You and Tommy go break something. You can have a bite later . . . if my students don't ruin the sauce."

Clarence came and went in the Navigator, dropping Nicky's father off somewhere and returning with an armful of party hats and horns for people to blow at midnight.

New Year's Eve! Nicky had almost forgotten what they were celebrating.

"Wow," Nicky said. "It's the last day of the year."

"So?" Tommy said. "What's for lunch?"

Nicky's mother flew into the room a short while later, full of energy and plans.

"I *must* run," she said. "I have a thousand things to do, and a meeting I'm late for now. Tommy, have you called your mother?"

Tommy looked ashamed. "No. I mean, I've called, but she's never answered."

"Call again," Nicky's mother said. "Keep calling until you reach her."

"Yes," Tommy said. "I will."

"I'll see you in a few hours. Nicholas, if your father calls, tell him I'll be out until this afternoon."

"Sure, Mom."

Tommy went to try to reach his mother. Nicky watched Grandma Tutti and her ladies work on their sauce.

"Some people chop the garlic," Grandma Tutti said to her students. "No! Not in my kitchen! We *mash* the garlic, gently, with the flat side of the knife. *Ecco!* Now you do it."

An hour later Nicky and Tommy were deep into a round of *BlackPlanet Two*.

"See?" Tommy said, just as his last space probe was blasted by the Astrogoths. "You have to double your shield strength, even if it means downgrading your tacticals. Then you get the tacticals back on the next screen."

Nicky stood up and said, "We have to go to the library."

"Right," Tommy said. "What are you talking about?"

"I Google'd Patrick Arlen this morning," Nicky said. "There're a lot of references to newspaper stories about him, but they're too old. You can't read them online. We have to go to the library to read the stories."

"They keep old newspapers in a library?"

"They have them on microfilm, and CDs," Nicky said. "My English class had a field trip. They showed us. Come on."

Nicky called Clarence and had him come around with the Navigator. At the front of the downtown library, he said, "We'll need about an hour. Can you pick us up at, like, five?"

"I'll be parked in front at five," Clarence said.

Inside, the library was deserted. The stacks of books stood tall and silent. Nicky stepped up to the reference desk, where a young woman with a tall hairdo was reading a thick, heavy-looking book.

"Excuse me," Nicky said. "I need to look something up in a newspaper."

"Guide to periodic literature," the woman said.

"Uh, okay," Nicky answered. "What does that mean?"

The woman said, "Follow me."

Nicky and Tommy sat at a long library table. In front of them was a big red book called the *Reader's Guide to Periodic Literature*—a bound directory of magazine and newspaper stories from the past.

"We'll never find him in all this!" Tommy whispered.

He started reading under the listings for *P*. Then he went back and started looking under the listings for *A*. Five minutes in, he suddenly said, "Here he is! Patrick Arlen."

The listing said, "Arlen, Patrick. 'Local Developer Missing.' *Ridgeway Register*. Nov. 13, 1982."

"What's that mean?" Tommy said.

"Beats me," Nicky answered. "We'd better ask."

The librarian directed the two boys to a computer terminal and sat them down. Then she returned with a CD-ROM and inserted it.

"This holds all the *Ridgeway Register* stories from 1975 to the present," she said. "Use the Search command to find the stories you need. Do you know how to do that?"

"Yes, ma'am," Nicky said.

He did as he was told. The disk booted up. Nicky performed a search on "Patrick Arlen." A dozen stories popped up. Nicky read the most recent one first.

The headline was LOCAL DEVELOPER MISSING. The story said, "Ridgeway real estate developer Patrick Arlen is missing and presumed dead, Comstock County Police Officer David Huckney said, after a weekend blaze that left Arlen's home in cinders. Huckney said an investigation into the cause of the blaze is under way. Fire officials, meanwhile, said that . . ."

"Wow," Tommy said. "Van Allen torched the guy's place and burned him to death."

"Murder!" Nicky said. "But who was Arlen?"

"Beats me," Tommy said. "Where's Ridgeway?"

"Down the shore," Nicky said. "About half as far as Newton."

"Read the next story," Tommy said.

The rest of the stories went back in time, all of them written by a reporter named Sean O'Farrell. One was about the fire. The one before that was about Arlen and his realty company declaring bankruptcy. The one before that was about Arlen being investigated for tax evasion, fraud and malfeasance.

"What's malfeasance?" Tommy said.

"I don't know," Nicky answered. "But it sounds bad."

The story before that was a big one about Arlen's real estate business and his alleged connection to organized crime.

"Check it out!" Tommy said. "He was a gangster!"

There was a picture, grainy and small. "He looks like a creep," Nicky said.

"He looks like a wiseguy," Tommy said. "Wait a minute! Is he one of the guys we saw at the amusement park? He looks familiar."

Nicky stared at the grainy picture. "He does, a little. But he's dead, remember?"

"Good riddance," Tommy said. "The guy was a crook."

Clarence was waiting for the boys outside when they left the library. He said, "Did you find what you were looking for?"

"Oh, yeah," Tommy said.

"So where are your books?"

"It was a reference book," Nicky said. "I just needed to take some notes."

Clarence dropped the boys in the driveway. Inside, the house smelled like heaven. Grandma Tutti had outdone herself. Even though Nicky's mother had hired a catering company to prepare food for the evening, Grandma Tutti had made a rack of meatballs, two huge lasagnas, several ricotta cheesecakes and another batch of *sfogliatella*. Now she was rolling out little rounds of dough for baby pizzas.

"Nicky, at last," she said. "I need someone to test the meatballs. I think they're too dry."

Nicky and Tommy flew to her side and found she was wrong. The meatballs were perfect.

"Good," Grandma Tutti said. "Now help me make the *pizzettas*."

Before dinner, Nicky went to his bedroom and looked up the *Ridgeway Register* in an online telephone book. When he had it, he turned on his cell phone and dialed.

"*Ridgeway Register*," a voice said. "How may I direct your call?"

"Uh, Mr. O'Farrell?"

"Hold on," the voice said. The phone rang twice and another voice said, "Yeah, O'Farrell."

"Hello?"

"Yeah, *hello*. We covered that already. Who is this?"

"This is Nicholas—uh, Smith. Ington. Smithington."

"Sure it is. And?"

Nicky took a breath. "And, and I'd like to ask you a

question about Patrick Arlen. I might have some information about his disappearance."

"Is that a fact?" Nicky could hear O'Farrell's heavy Irish accent. He sounded like the leprechaun on the Lucky Charms commercials. "Well, let me think. If I remember correctly, Mr. Arlen disappeared about twenty years ago. Is this new information?"

"I don't know," Nicky said. "But I think Patrick Arlen was murdered. And I think I know who did it."

"Great John O'Groats!" O'Farrell said. "That *is* interesting. Would you come down to the paper and talk to me about it?"

"I don't know," Nicky said. "I want to, but I have to be careful."

"Why is that, son? Are you in some kind of danger?"

"No, but someone I know might be—from the same person who I think killed Patrick Arlen."

"Okay, laddie," O'Farrell said. "Listen to me. It's New Year's Eve, or it will be shortly. I'm leaving the office. But tomorrow, or anytime after, if you want to stop by the office and chat, I'll be here. It's Sean O'Farrell, at the *Register*. You won't forget that, will you?"

"No, sir."

"All right then," the leprechaun said. "Ta-ta for now."

Nicky hung up. His palms were sweaty and he felt a little dizzy. Was he making a mistake talking to some newspaper reporter about this?

He didn't know. But he didn't know what choice he

had. He needed more information before he could go to the police. He needed to know who Arlen was, and if Peter Van Allen really killed him. He also needed to know, for sure, that his dad wasn't doing anything against the law. He wanted to get rid of Peter Van Allen if he was a criminal. But what if he got his dad in trouble at the same time?

That was why he had to see O'Farrell. He had the information. And the reporter couldn't go to the police unless Nicky told him the whole story . . . which Nicky didn't have to do until O'Farrell agreed to help.

Nicky told Tommy everything O'Farrell had said.

"Do you know this guy?" Tommy asked. "Can we trust him?"

"I don't know," Nicky said. "But we have to go see him. For now, let's just keep our eyes open. And keep quiet."

The Borellis' guests started arriving around seven. By eight, the Borelli house was filled. Here came Jimmy the Iceman, Charlie Cement, Oscar the Undertaker, Bobby Car Service and of course Sal Carmenza, with wife and daughter. Donna was wearing a black velvet dress, and her hair was up. To Nicky, it was like he'd never seen her before. He'd known she was pretty, but *wow*. She looked so grown-up that he got shy and tongue-tied when he said hello to her. That funny feeling returned to his stomach.

"Uh, hi," he said.

"Uh, hi," she said back, and laughed. "Uh, what's wrong with you?"

"Uh, nothing. I mean, nothing," Nicky said. "Can I get you a soda?"

"Uh, yeah!" Donna said, and laughed again. "Where's your hoodlum?"

"My *what?*" Nicky asked. "Oh. I think Tommy's still getting dressed."

Nicky took Donna to the back of the living room, where the caterers had set up a bar, and got her a soda. He showed her the tent in his backyard. Then he stood with his hands in his pockets and found he had nothing to say.

Luckily Donna had plenty. The marathon poker game had gone on so late, the owners of the bed-and-breakfast had told the Brooklyn men they were going to call the police. Uncle Frankie had had to tell them he *was* the police to calm them down.

Then, the next morning, the whole gang had sat down for breakfast. The Brooklyn men had eaten so many pancakes that the owners had run out of pancake batter. They'd never seen people who ate so much.

"Your uncle was laughing so hard I thought he was going to die," Donna said.

Across the room, Uncle Frankie was laughing now as Charlie Cement retold the pancake-eating-marathon story to Nicky's father.

"I'm never going to be able to show my face in Newton again," Nicky's father said. "You guys have ruined my reputation."

"Now he's got a reputation!" Jimmy the Iceman said. "Mr. Big Stuff!"

"Well, look at this house," Oscar the Undertaker said. "What do you do here, Nick—rent rooms? This is bigger than the place you got us staying in."

"Nicer, too," Charlie Cement said. "And I bet every bedroom has its own bathroom. How come we don't get to stay here?"

"Nick don't want to trash the joint up with bums like you," Jimmy said. "This is only for classy people."

"That can't be right," Sallie said. "Frankie's stayin' here."

"Watch it, you," Frankie said.

"Seriously, guys, you're welcome," Nicky's father said. "I'm really touched to have you all in my home."

"You're gonna get touched, all right, with a place like this," Oscar said. "I'd like to hit you up for a couple of *hunge* right now."

"You must be doin' all right for yourself," Jimmy said. "This ain't exactly Bath Avenue!"

Nicky's father looked embarrassed. "Oh, it's just a house. What difference does it make where you live? It's just a place to eat and sleep and hang your hat, right?"

"That's the truth, Nick," Sallie the Butcher said. "And you're a swell guy to invite us all up here. Right, guys?"

"You bet," Jimmy said. "Now, where's the wine?"

"There you go," Charlie said. "It always ends up being about the wine with you."

"Aha," Donna said. "Finally. Here comes Tommy."

Nicky had no idea where he'd been hiding it, but Tommy was dressed in a suit. His hair was slicked back.

95

He was wearing a dress shirt with an open collar, and shiny black shoes with pointy toes.

"Whoa," Donna said. "Look at you!"

"What?" Tommy said, and ran his hand over his hair. "Can't a guy get dressed up?"

"I'm impressed," Donna said. "You look nice."

"Nice," Tommy said, and scowled. "That's bad, when someone says you look *nice*. You don't like the suit?"

"I think you look great," Nicky said. "Were you hiding that in your little bag?"

"What else?" Tommy said. "I brought it with me for the party."

"Lookin' good," Nicky said. "So who's it for?"

Tommy's face got red. "None of your business."

"Okay," Nicky said, and laughed. "But relax. She's not here yet."

Then, half an hour later, she was. Amy came through the front door with her mother, Marian. Nicky watched Tommy's face get red again. He also watched his uncle Frankie's face light up.

"Marian!" Frankie said. "Mrs. Galloway! Come and meet my friends from Brooklyn. Guys, this is the lady I told you about. Meet Marian."

"Hi," Amy said to Nicky. "By which I mean, can you imagine anything more boring in your life than a grown-up New Year's Eve party? They're all going to get drunk. At midnight the lights will go out and they'll play kissy-face for ten minutes."

"That might not be so bad," Tommy said, and winked. "Depends who you're kissing, right? Maybe you'll get lucky."

"Oh dear," Amy said. "Are you trying to be, like, *sexy* or something?"

"I don't have to try," Tommy said. "It comes naturally. Come on. Show me how you dance."

Nicky winced. If there ever had been a girl who would hate being talked to like that, it was Amy. To his surprise, though, she laughed at Tommy and said, "Okay. Maybe I *will*."

They walked off together.

The music was thumping. Nicky thought about all the moves Tommy had taught him. He could show them to Donna. But suddenly he was too nervous even to try them.

"I'm kinda hungry—are you?" Nicky said.

"Kinda," Donna said. "Are those your grandmother's meatballs I see over there?"

"Yeah."

"Let's go."

The night seemed to last forever. More and more guests arrived. The house got fuller, and louder. Father David came to the party with three old ladies Nicky recognized as his grandmother's friends from St. Monica's. The wine flowed. People moved out under the tent and started dancing. Some of the grown-ups got a little tipsy. Wild laughter rang out now and then. Sometimes Donna could tell who it was. "Bobby Car Service," she would say, or, "That's Oscar the Undertaker's wife. She likes to drink."

Around ten o'clock, Nicky saw his mother in a corner talking with a man in a dark suit over a dark turtleneck. Nicky realized with a jolt that it was the same man he'd seen talking with his mother in the backyard. What was he doing *here*? Nicky looked around for Tommy, and for Uncle Frankie, and for his father. They were all someplace else. He wanted to tell Donna about it. But he also didn't.

He decided not to think about it. He got a cold drink and went back to where he'd left Donna.

Nicky's friends Chad and Jordan came with their parents. They didn't dance. They didn't eat. They couldn't wait to leave.

Tommy and Amy danced for hours. They danced fast. They danced slow. They danced cheek to cheek. Tommy was doing the box step!

A little while later, he took a break and said to Nicky, "I haven't seen you out there. What's the deal?"

"Just don't feel like it, I guess," Nicky said. "I've been talking to Donna."

"*Talking* to her? Dance with her!"

"Maybe in a while," Nicky said.

Around ten-thirty, just as Nicky and Donna were going back to the bar for another cold drink, the door opened. There, with a blast of chilly air, were Peter Van Allen, his wife and their son, Dirk.

Nicky couldn't run. He couldn't hide. He said, "Oh, good evening, Mr. Van Allen, Mrs. Van Allen. Come in."

"Hello, young man," Mr. Van Allen said, nodding at Nicky and Donna. "And young lady. We're sorry to arrive so late, and unfortunately we can't stay. We just dropped by to wish your parents a happy new year. Say hello, Dirk."

"Hello, Nicholas," Dirk said in a singsong voice. "Are you having a happy new year?"

"The best," Nicky said. "I'll go get my mom and dad."

Nicky got his mom, found his dad and told them that the Van Allens were there.

Tommy was standing in the living room, staring at Peter Van Allen. Nicky whispered, "What's wrong?"

"It's so weird," Tommy whispered. "Like, we might be looking at a killer. He doesn't look dangerous at all."

"Well, stop staring," Nicky said, and then noticed Peter Van Allen looking at them. He cleared his throat and said, "I'm going to see if Donna's okay."

He found Donna again and was about to ask her if she wanted to try a dance when he saw Dirk Van Allen coming across the living room. Dirk looked angry. Nicky turned to see where he was going. He was heading for the backyard. Through the window, Nicky could see Amy and Tommy slow dancing under the tent.

Nicky got there about the same time Dirk did. The music had just ended. Tommy and Amy were clapping.

Dirk said, "You. You're a dead man. And you, come on. You're leaving."

"I'm not going anywhere," Amy said.

"You're leaving *now*," Dirk said. "And I'm taking care of *you* later."

"Anytime you want, including right here and right now," Tommy said. "But she's staying."

"Listen to me, you little Brooklyn—"

"You've tented the whole thing!" a loud voice said behind them.

They all turned. Nicky's father and mother were leading the Van Allens on a tour of the tented backyard.

"Are the heaters electric?" Mrs. Van Allen asked.

"Gas," Nicky's father said. "Very powerful, too."

"I *feel* it," she said. "And look at everyone dancing! What a marvelous party!"

"We were just going inside, actually," Nicky said. "We're going to get a little more punch."

"Yeah, Dirk," Tommy said. "How'd *you* like a little punch?"

"None for me!" Peter Van Allen said. "We've already drunk the legal limit. Come, Dirk. Any more 'punch' and *you'll* have to drive us home. Say good night to your friends."

Dirk turned to Nicky and Tommy. He gritted his teeth and made a sound like a dog growling.

"Good night, Dirky," Tommy said. "See you soo-oon."

Midnight came. The adults all grabbed hats and hooters. They held hands. They turned off the music. They all started counting down: "Ten. Nine. Eight. Seven. Six . . ."

Tommy and Amy had disappeared. Nicky smiled weakly at Donna, who reached over and took his hand.

"Three! Two! One!"

The lights went out. Horns blew. Hooters hooted. Someone screamed. Music started: "Should old ac-quain-tance be for-got . . ."

And there, in the dark, in the crowd of yelling, hooting adults, Nicky felt something warm and sweet on his cheek. A kiss! He almost fainted. Instead, he hugged Donna. Soon they were dancing to "Auld Lang Syne."

Chapter
8

Early the next morning, Nicky was in the kitchen helping his grandma Tutti make *zeppoli*. They were rolling out the dough when Uncle Frankie stumbled into the room.

"Happy new year," he said in a grumpy voice, and gave Grandma Tutti a kiss.

"You're here early," Grandma Tutti said.

"I'm here *late*," Frankie said. "I stayed up half the night and slept on the couch. You got coffee?"

"I'll make coffee."

Nicky went outside to get the newspaper and came back clapping his hands together from the cold. Frankie sipped his coffee and read the headlines.

"Look at this," he said. "Your old man made the news. There's something about his real estate thing."

Nicky's heart began to pound. Then he looked at the headline: REDEVELOPMENT PLAN FOR FAIRPORT. He relaxed and read the beginning of the story: "A team of investors headed by Peter Van Allen and local lawyer Nicholas Borelli has obtained financing to turn historic downtown Fairport into a haven for artists and middle-income metro families. By Monday, the new condominium project . . ."

Frankie, reading over his shoulder, said, "You know what's interesting? They say who your dad is, but they only give Van Allen's name. Why's that?"

"Nobody needs to be told who Peter Van Allen is," Nicky said. "You just say the name."

"So your old man gets second billing," Frankie said. "Hey, there's also something in here about that dance of yours, that Snow Cone thing."

"Snow Ball," Nicky said. "It's Sunday night."

"You got a date?"

"Donna, I guess," Nicky said, "if her parents will let her."

"And what about Tommy?" Grandma Tutti asked. "Who's he gonna ask?"

"He's going with Amy Galloway," Nicky said. "*She* asked *him*, last night, at midnight."

"Whoa!" Frankie said. "These Carrington girls are pretty fast!"

"Not all of them," Nicky said. "Just Amy."

"And her mother," Frankie said. "She asked *me*."

"To the Snow Ball?"

"Yeah. I said yes."

"So you can double-date," Grandma Tutti said. "Now get up and come help me, Nicky. The oil's hot. We gotta fry the *zeppoli*."

"I'm sorry to miss 'em, but I gotta go," Frankie said. On his way out, he added, "Hey, Nicky D, don't let your folks be late tonight, right? They get there after seven, all the food'll be gone."

"Okay," Nicky said.

Tommy got up a little while later and came downstairs. Grandma Tutti served him a *zeppoli* and said, "You boys take that in the other room. I have a lot to do in here."

Nicky took Tommy into the breakfast room. He said, "Look at this," and showed him the newspaper story. "It says 'by Monday,' right?"

"So?"

Nicky looked up to make sure no one was listening. "So if that's when the Fairport thing is going to go down, then my dad could be in danger *now*."

"Why?" Tommy said. "Oh! You mean, like Van Allen might try to get him out of the way or something."

"Yeah," Nicky said. "Or something. I think we have to try to talk to that newspaper reporter. Like, now."

"He said you could call, right?"

"Or go to the paper."

"Call, then," Tommy said. "See if he's there."

Nicky's mother came through the library as he was dialing. She said, "Where's your uncle?"

"Gone, I think," Nicky said. "He said goodbye."

"Who're you talking to?"

"I was leaving a message for Chad," Nicky said. "He's not there. I'm going to call Jordan now. We're going to ride the bus to the mall."

"All right," his mother said. "But remember, you have to be back this afternoon early enough for us to go to Newton. And don't stay on the phone too long. I'm expecting a call."

Nicky finished dialing when she left, then said into the phone, "Mr. O'Farrell?"

Two minutes later, he put the phone down. He went back to the breakfast room.

"So?"

"I left a message. I left my cell number."

"Cool," Tommy said. "Now we can hang out!"

"What do you want to do?"

"I don't know. Whatta you got?"

"We could play laser tag."

"All right!" Tommy said. "What's laser tag?"

"Let me see if Clarence can drive us to the mall, and I'll show you."

An hour later, Nicky was showing him.

"You put on this vest. It's got these electronic things on it. If someone shoots you, it lights up. You're dead, and your gun won't work for, like, fifteen seconds. Then you can start shooting again."

Nicky handed Tommy a vest and put on his own. "So what's the point?" Tommy said.

"It's like this giant dark room," Nicky said. "With stairs, and walls, and fake boulders. You and me are a team. We have to defeat the other teams."

"Who's the other teams?"

"Whoever's in there already," Nicky said. "Come on!"

It took a second for their eyes to adjust to the dark. At first, Nicky and Tommy could see only red laser blasts around them. Then the shapes of walls and rocks and stairways appeared.

"C'mon," Nicky whispered. "Follow me."

They were ambushed in the first room. A voice said, "Get 'em!" and the air was filled with red laser blasts. Nicky's and Tommy's vests lit up, and the voice said, "Blasted!" Nicky and Tommy dropped to the ground and waited fifteen seconds for their vests to stop blinking.

"Okay," Nicky said. "Let's crawl around this way and get them."

For an hour they ran, hid, blasted, got blasted in return and shouted until their voices were hoarse. At the end of the hour, their lasers went dead. Nicky said, "Time's up. C'mon."

They turned in the equipment and went out to the food court. "We can steal some more of that lemonade," Tommy said.

"It's free refills, actually," Nicky said.

Tommy looked disappointed. "Free? I stole all those drinks for nothing?"

"Yeah. Kinda. Listen, did you ever do paintball?"

"No."

"Me neither. I want to do paintball."

"Me too," Tommy said. "What's that?"

That was Walter Wager, from Nicky's school. He was jogging down the center of the mall, carrying four or five large bags from the department store, in a hurry. Chasing him were three other kids, led by Dirk Van Allen. One kid punched a hole in one of Walter's bags. Something fell out. Walter bent down to pick it up. Another kid grabbed Walter's shoelaces and untied them. Walter said, "Cut it out!" and set his bags down to tie his shoes. The third kid kicked one of Walter's bags like it was a soccer ball. It skidded down the mall while Walter cried out, "No! Stop it!"

Then Dirk grabbed him and tugged at his pants from behind. Walter was standing in the middle of the Carrington Mall with his shoes untied, his packages scattered all around him, and tears started to stream down his face.

Dirk was cackling madly. "Boo hoo, Wally," he said as he swatted Wally's backside. "Boo hoo hoo."

"That's it." Tommy was moving before Nicky could stop him.

He ran across the mall, Nicky chasing him, and planted himself in front of Dirk. "How about fighting someone who can fight back, huh?" he said. "How about that?"

Dirk didn't put his fists up. Instead, he grinned strangely and said, "Gee, let me think about it for a second."

Nicky saw why. He shouted, "Tommy! Look out!" but it was too late. Dirk's three friends came at Tommy from behind. The first slugged him in the back of the head just as the second dove into the backs of his knees. Tommy went down hard. Then all four boys were on top of him.

Tommy could handle Dirk, but Nicky knew he was no match for Dirk and three friends, even if Nicky helped. He ran back to the lemonade stand and said, "Call security! Quick!"

The security men were already on their way, running down the mall, shouting and blowing whistles. They pulled the boys away from each other.

Tommy's jeans were ripped, and one of his shoes was missing, but otherwise he looked okay.

"We're taking you in," the security man said.

"Why me?" Dirk said. "I didn't do anything! This guy went crazy and attacked me. My friends were just trying to get him off me."

The two security men looked at each other. They hadn't seen what had happened. But they knew Dirk Van Allen and his friends—and his father.

And they'd never seen Tommy before. One security man said to Dirk, "Okay. Take off." Then he looked at Tommy. "You, come with me."

Nicky's mother and father were *not* happy. They sat in the den with the two boys. The sun had gone down. From somewhere in the house, a clock chimed five times. Nicky's father sighed deeply.

"We talked about this over the summer, Tommy," he said. "I can't have you dragging Nicholas into this kind of violence."

"Dad, he didn't drag *me* into—"

"Don't interrupt your father," Nicky's mother said.

"But we—"

"Nicholas!" his mother said. "It's bad enough that this has happened. You're making it worse by inventing a story about Tommy rescuing some boy who was being beaten up."

"But, Mom! It's true! Walter—"

"We went over this with the security people at the mall," she said. "They said there was no other boy involved."

"You're just lucky the people over there know me," Nicky's father said to Tommy. "Otherwise they might have turned you over to the police. Assault is no laughing matter around here."

The doorbell rang. Nicky's mother looked at her watch and said, "Now who could *that* be?"

Nicky's father said, "Don't move. I'm not finished with you."

He came back in a moment. Behind him were a man and a woman Nicky didn't recognize. Behind *them* was Walter Wager.

"We've come to thank Nicky's friend for stepping in and helping our son today," the man said. "It's Tommy, isn't it? You're the boy from Brooklyn?"

Tommy, looking nervously at Nicky's father, nodded.

"Well, thank you," the man said. "What you did today was quite heroic. Are you feeling all right?"

Tommy nodded. "They didn't really get me."

"Who didn't?" Nicky's father asked. "Maybe you'd better explain what happened."

"My son Walter here was being pushed around by that Dirk Van Allen and some of his friends," the man said. "Tommy jumped in and made them stop. One boy against four. That's real bravery."

"Or stupidity," Nicky's father said. "I didn't realize . . . That is, the boys were just explaining what happened."

"He deserves a commendation," Walter's father said. "Or at the very least, a token of our appreciation. I don't know if you're familiar with the Bookworm, in Canfield, but that's our store. I have a couple of gift certificates here for you boys. I hope you'll come by and pick something out for yourselves."

Walter's father presented Nicky and Tommy with matching envelopes that said *The Bookworm* on the outside.

"Thank you both, again," the man said. "Thank you for watching out for my boy. Walter, don't you have something to say?"

"Yeah, thanks," Walter said, staring at the floor. "I mean, you know, like—thanks."

"*Fugheddaboudit,*" Tommy said.

Walter looked up from the floor and said, "Huh?"

"He means, 'no problem,' " Nicky said.

When the Wagers had gone, Nicky's father said, "I'm not sure that makes things any different. Fighting is fighting, even if the other guys start it. I don't ever want to have this conversation again—understand?"

Both boys nodded.

"All right," he said. "Now let's see if we can get down to the party before those animals have devoured all the food."

Nicky and his parents, with Grandma Tutti and Tommy, got to the Newton bed-and-breakfast well before seven. The food wasn't gone yet. In fact, the guys from Brooklyn had laid on a feast. There were a ham and a roast beef. There were prosciutto and mozzarella. There were regular lasagna and spinach lasagna. There were baskets of bread and jugs of wine. Everyone seemed to be eating and drinking—a lot.

Nicky had never seen anything like it. He'd never seen grown-ups have this kind of fun. Parties in Carrington were always very polite. These grown-ups appeared to be really enjoying themselves.

Charlie Cement had taken a lampshade off a lamp and was pretending that it was a sombrero. He was singing the "Mexican Hat Dance" and skipping around the room. Jimmy the Iceman was trying to slow dance with his girlfriend, Janice, but she was trying to finish a conversation with Sallie the Butcher's wife—Donna's mother. When Bobby Car Service noticed that there was a piano in the parlor, he started playing it. Everyone gathered around and listened tearfully while he sang " 'O Sole Mio" in Italian, and then they laughed while he sang "That's Amore" just like Dean Martin.

Nicky, sitting with Donna and Tommy, said, "How often do they get like this?"

"Just for special occasions," Donna said.

"New Year's Day, Columbus Day, Friday . . . ," Tommy said. "Unless it's my mom, in which case it's every day."

After the food was all gone, Oscar the Undertaker made a speech. Charlie Cement proposed a toast. Uncle Frankie told Nicky's father he loved him. Grandma Tutti cried. Nicky's father said, "I think this is the start of a wonderful new year. I wish each and every one of you all the health and happiness in the world. My only resolution is to see more of you all, more often. To the happy new year!"

"Happy new year!" everyone shouted, and raised their glasses.

It was late when the party broke up. Nicky and Tommy fell asleep in the car going home. When they arrived, they stumbled out of the car and up the stairs to Nicky's bedroom.

But then Nicky had trouble falling asleep. Too much had happened. Too much was going on. He felt like he had a lot to worry about. He heard Tommy shifting around in bed, too.

"You can't sleep, either, huh?" Nicky said. "Does your head hurt?"

"A little," Tommy said. "One of those guys really smacked me."

"It looked like it," Nicky said. "I hate to think what would've happened if those security guys hadn't come."

"Are you kidding? I woulda *killed* them guys. What I wouldn't give to see 'em again."

"You might get another chance, at the Snow Ball," Nicky said. "Maybe we should think about not going."

Tommy rose up on one elbow and looked at Nicky. "Why not?"

"Well, you know Dirk is going to be there, with his friends. Now that we know who his dad really is, maybe we should stay out of his way."

"Wow," Tommy said. "I completely forgot about that. He could have us whacked."

The boys thought about that for a minute. Then Tommy said, "But that's stupid. No one's going to whack a couple of teenagers in public, in a place like Carrington, at a thing like the Snow Ball. Right?"

"Right," Nicky said. "Right?"

"Right," Tommy said. "Besides, you already invited Donna, and I already agreed to take Amy. We gotta show up, or we'll look like weenies . . . which is worse than getting whacked."

Chapter
9

The boys from Brooklyn had all gone home. Sallie the Butcher had agreed to let Donna come back to Carrington for the Snow Ball but had decided to take her back to Brooklyn until then.

That morning Frankie was up early again. He found Grandma Tutti in the kitchen drinking coffee and kneading dough.

"Morning, Ma," he said. "You making bread?"

"No, I'm making meat loaf," she said. "What does it look like?"

"I don't know, Ma. You know me and cooking."

"I know you and *eating*. Where are you going so early? Don't you have time for breakfast?"

"No, Ma," Frankie said, and kissed Grandma Tutti on the cheek. "I said I'd go into town and meet Nick."

Grandma Tutti beamed. "My boys! Together again! Are you going to come work for him?"

"Don't be ridiculous," Frankie said. "He just wants to show me his building. So I gotta go shave."

Nicky and Tommy woke up while Frankie was getting ready. They went downstairs to the smells of baking bread and frying bacon. Grandma Tutti was working at the stove.

"How do you want your eggs?" she asked.

"Scrambled," Nicky said.

"Me too," Tommy said.

"Sit," Grandma Tutti said.

Just then Nicky's cell phone rang. He dashed from the room to take the call.

"This is Sean O'Farrell," a man with an Irish accent said to him. "I'm returning a call to this number."

"Yes, thank you," Nicky said. "I want to come talk to you about that Patrick Arlen thing."

"Well, come, then," the reporter said. "The press never sleeps."

"I can be there in an hour or two," Nicky said.

"Ta-ta for now, then."

Nicky hung up and met his father coming into the kitchen. "You're taking calls pretty early," he said. "Try to keep it down, okay? Your mother's not feeling well."

"What's wrong with her?" Nicky asked.

"Probably a cold," his father answered. "Maybe she's tired. She just wants to sleep in."

"If she'd eat my chicken soup, I'd have her up in an hour," Grandma Tutti said.

"Don't start, Ma, please," Nicky's father said. "What do you boys have cooked up for the day?"

"Nothing, yet," Nicky said. "I wish it wasn't so cold. We can't really ride bikes, or skate, or do anything out of doors."

"Maybe you should go to Canfield, to that bookstore."

"Maybe," Nicky said.

"Or you should work on your dance moves," his father said, and winked.

Nicky blushed. "Dad! How did—"

"I'm sorry," his father said. "I shouldn't kid you about it, but Clarence told me you guys were working up some kind of routine."

"I just wanted to learn to dance a little."

"I think it's great," his father said. "Me, I never learned how to dance. Frankie's a great dancer—a natural. But I was always too shy. To this day, except for two minutes at my wedding, I've never danced a step."

"It was a beautiful wedding," Grandma Tutti said. "Not like Frankie's, since it wasn't all Italian—but beautiful."

"If I live to be a hundred, I'll never hear the end of this," Nicky's father said. "Try to remember you're a guest in my house, Ma. Try to be nice."

"I am trying," Grandma Tutti said. "This is the best I can do."

"Try harder," Nicky's father said. "And tell your favorite

son, if he ever comes down here, that I'm warming up the car."

After breakfast, Nicky said, "I'm gonna go up and see Mom."

"Ask her if she wants some breakfast," Grandma Tutti said.

Nicky found her sitting in bed, in dim light, with a book on her lap, and her eyes closed. Nicky looked and then started to leave.

"Nicky? What's wrong?"

He went to her. "Nothing, Mom. I just came up to see how you were doing. Grandma wants to know if you want breakfast."

"I'm fine," she said. "But no breakfast. I might get up for lunch."

"Could I bring it up here? Or get you some tea or something?"

"You're sweet," she said, and smiled. She seemed so weak. And sick. She was never sick. Seeing her like this was scary to Nicky.

"Do you think you've got a cold?" he asked.

"Probably," she said, and closed her eyes. "Which I don't have time for. I have a million things to do."

"You've had a lot going on," he said. "With Christmas, and New Year's and all the other stuff."

"You don't know the half of it," she said. Then she opened her eyes. "What other stuff?"

Had he said too much? Nicky panicked. "I don't know. It just seems like you've got a lot going on."

"Never you mind about that," his mother said. She didn't sound sick anymore. She sounded like Mom. "You have enough to worry about without concerning yourself with my little affairs. Now, go downstairs and see if you can help your grandmother. And make sure that Tommy calls his mother."

Back in the breakfast room, he said, "My mom says call your mom."

"Okay," Tommy said. "Then what? Who was that on the phone?"

"It was him," Nicky whispered. "I said we'd be there in an hour."

"What's all that whispering?" Grandma Tutti asked.

"I think we should call Chad and go to Canfield," Tommy said in a too-loud voice. "I'll just call my mom first."

"Yes," Nicky said. "That's a good idea. I'll get dressed."

Twenty minutes later, the two boys were bundled up and trudging up the road to the bus stop.

Nicky said, "So what did your mom say?"

"She said I could stay for the party, but I gotta go home Monday," Tommy said. "School starts Tuesday morning! I can't believe it."

"Mine too. Christmas went by so fast."

"Everything good goes by too fast," Tommy said.

It took another thirty-five minutes for the boys to get to Ridgeway, a sleepy town that had been a big city at the turn of the century but was now mostly closed factories and boarded-up buildings. Nicky and Tommy walked down the main street until they found the *Ridgeway Register*—

in a big brick building with the year "1827" stamped over the doorway.

"Here goes nothing," Nicky said.

Tommy followed him inside.

A janitor was sweeping the huge old lobby. He pointed at the ceiling and said, "Second floor."

An ancient elevator left Nicky and Tommy in a vast open room filled with desks and chairs. On some of the desks there were computer monitors. On others there were old typewriters. From the far corner came a small wide man with curly yellow hair and a curly yellow beard.

"Come in, come in," he called to them. "You're welcome."

Sean O'Farrell introduced himself and shook the boys' hands. Nicky said, "I'm Nicholas, and this is my friend."

"Welcome to the *Ridgeway Register*. This was a busy newspaper when I arrived in nineteen fifty-three. Every one of these desks was occupied. Then, one by one, the reporters lost their jobs. Now I write the paper almost single-handedly. It's a little busier than this during the week—but not much. Pull up a chair."

Nicky told his story carefully. He said he had reason to believe that Patrick Arlen had been murdered, and he was almost certain that he knew who had done it. But he needed more information before he went to the police.

"I should think so," O'Farrell said. "Murder is a serious charge. What information do you need?"

"Well, anything," Nicky said. "Did the police have any suspects?"

"They thought it was a mob hit," O'Farrell said. "Arlen was in business with some shady characters, of the Cosa Nostra variety—the Mafia, in other words. When someone doing business with them disappears, you usually assume they didn't just go on holiday."

"So you think the gangsters killed him in that fire?"

"The police said it was 'of a suspicious nature,' but they never called it arson," O'Farrell said. "And they never found Arlen's body. Too bad. He was a good-lookin' fella, and he would've made a good-lookin' corpse. After your telephone call, I went through my old files. Here's his picture."

It was the same photograph that Nicky and Tommy had seen in the library. But it wasn't small and dark and grainy. It was a big 8 x 10. Nicky took one look at it and gasped.

"What?" Tommy said, and grabbed the picture out of Nicky's hands. "Wow! It's Dirk! It looks like an older version of Dirk!"

"Not exactly," Nicky said. "It's a younger version of his dad."

It took Nicky a few minutes to collect his thoughts, catch his breath and tell Sean O'Farrell his story. And first he had to swear the reporter to secrecy. "You have to promise, but *promise*, that you won't tell anybody about this until I'm sure my dad is safe," he said.

"Trust me to keep a secret," O'Farrell said. "But *you* have to promise that you won't tell this story to any other reporter. I want the exclusive. Do we have a deal?"

"We have a deal," Nicky said. "But what do I do now?"

"It's a bit tricky," the reporter said, and put his feet up on his desk. "You can't let this Peter Van Allen know that you know he's really Patrick Arlen. And you can't talk to the police until you've made sure your dad's in the clear. Am I right?"

"Right," Nicky said.

"You'd best let me investigate," O'Farrell said. "See what I can find out about this Van Allen, without bringing Mr. Arlen back from the dead."

"Can you do that?"

"I'm a newspaper man!" the reporter said. "I've a license to stir things up. Let me snoop around a bit."

"Okay, but can you do it fast?"

O'Farrell smiled. "I work for a daily newspaper. I do everything fast. But what's the rush?"

"This real estate deal in Fairport is supposed to be finished on Monday," Nicky said. "I heard my dad say they were going to sign the papers then. I just have this bad feeling that if Van Allen is going to do something, he might do it soon."

"I understand entirely," O'Farrell said. "You're a good lad to worry so about your poor old father."

Nicky shrugged and looked at the floor, like it was nothing, but his eyes filled with tears.

"I'm just afraid something bad is going to happen," he said.

"Now, now, you've nothing to worry about," O'Farrell

said. "Trust me. I'll see that no harm comes to you. Or to your poor old father. *Trust me*."

As they rode the bus along the snowy streets, back to Carrington, Tommy said, "Are we making a mistake? That guy gives me the creeps."

"He's a newspaper reporter," Nicky said. "I think he's on the level."

"Really?" Tommy asked. "I remember my own mother telling me, 'Never trust a man who says "Trust me" more than once.' It's my mother, I know, but that guy said it about ten times."

"I think he's okay," Nicky said. "I have a good feeling about him."

When the two boys had gone, Sean O'Farrell sat with his feet on the desk for a while, considering their strange story. Patrick Arlen reborn as Peter Van Allen? Who'd believe such a tall tale? He tried to imagine the headlines. Carrington's leading citizen unmasked as a former Mafia errand boy?

When he was finished laughing about that, he pulled a tattered reporter's notebook out of his desk and thumbed through it until he found a phone number. He dialed and waited.

Then he said, "Mr. Van Allen? It's your old friend Sean O'Farrell, down at the *Ridgeway Register*."

There was a long, silent pause. Then O'Farrell said, "Yes, it has been a long time. I'm calling because I've got a little story for you—and it's a corker. It involves two fellas who've identified you as Patrick Arlen."

O'Farrell listened for a moment, then interrupted. "Mr. Van Allen, I didn't say I had a story for my newspaper. I said I have a story for *you*. The only question is, what's it worth?"

O'Farrell listened for another moment, then said, "Oh, I think it's worth quite a bit, Mr. Van Allen. But you think it over. And I'll hang on to the names of these two fellas while you do. Ta-ta for now."

O'Farrell hung up. He thought, *If the phone rings again very shortly, that means he's going to pay me to be quiet. If it doesn't, that means he's going to pay someone else to* make *me be quiet—permanently. I wonder which it will be. . . .*

He didn't wonder long. The phone rang. The reporter picked it up and said, "Yeah, O'Farrell." He listened, smiled and said, "That's a very generous offer, Mr. Van Allen. I'll take it."

Nicky's mom was sitting in the library when the boys went in through the front door. She said, "Where in the world have you been? I tried your cell and got no answer. And Chad's mother said—"

"We went without those guys, Mom," Nicky said. "Then the bus—"

"Well, never mind," his mother said. "Go get cleaned up. I'll tell your grandmother that you're back. I just heard from your father. He and Frankie are on their way home now."

"Okay," Nicky said. "And I'm glad you're feeling better."

The boys had time for a round of *BlackPlanet Two*. Sometime near dusk, Nicky glanced out his bedroom window while Tommy was making his play, and noticed someone moving around in the backyard. Nicky went to the window and looked out.

Below him, in the dim light, was a man in black jeans, black boots, a black parka and a black ski hat. He was studying the back of the house. He slipped behind some trees. He ducked behind the pool house. He seemed to be staring at the upstairs windows.

"Tommy!" Nicky whispered, and dropped to his knees. "C'mere!"

Tommy squatted next to him. "What?"

"There's a guy in the backyard. See him?"

Tommy looked. "Maybe it's the gardener."

"Tommy! I know what the gardener looks like."

"What about the, like, pool guy?"

"Does that guy look like the pool guy?"

"No," Tommy said. "He looks like a burglar. He's casing the joint."

"No!" Nicky said. "What does that mean—casing the joint?"

"He's figuring out how to break in, and how to escape with the stuff," Tommy said. "Look at how he's dressed. He's a real pro."

"What do we do?"

"How should I know? Call your uncle?"

"Yeah!" Nicky grabbed his cell phone out of his backpack. "No! Wait! What if—"

"It doesn't matter," Tommy said. "He's gone. He was there, and then he wasn't there."

"Listen!" Nicky said. "That's a car starting."

The boys stared at the snow-covered backyard.

"Wow," Nicky said. "You don't think he could be one of the guys we saw at the amusement park, do you?"

"Maybe. Why?"

" 'Cause what if they know we heard them? What if they know that we know what they're going to do?"

"So, what if?"

"Well, wouldn't they want to, you know, uh, like, *take care* of us?"

"Get outta here!" Tommy said, and laughed. "That's ridiculous."

The two boys stared at the yard.

"At least I *think* it's ridiculous," Tommy said.

Nicky's dad and Uncle Frankie were back. The house was filled with noise again. The living room smelled like food. Dinner was wonderful.

"Nicky, have you and Tommy seen the Fairport thing?" Frankie asked.

"Uh, yeah, sort of," Nicky said. "Just the outside."

"It's gonna be huge," Frankie said. "You start with the housing, get those artists in there, bring in your Starbucks and your Sbarro—I'm telling you, it's gonna be huge. Where do I sign up to invest?"

125

Nicky's father laughed. "You'll have to talk to Van Allen," he said. "He's the bankroll. I'm just the brains."

"Just the brains!" Grandma Tutti said. "Listen to Senator Borelli—modest all of a sudden!"

After dinner and a bad TV movie, the boys went up to Nicky's bedroom. Lying in the dark, Tommy asked again if Nicky thought Sean O'Farrell was going to protect him.

"I think so," Nicky said. "But you never know with grown-ups."

"Tell me about it," Tommy said. "I never know whether my mom is telling me the truth or not."

"I know," Nicky said. "It's like they've got one story for their kids and another story for the adults. Like my mom, with the guy we saw at the mall. She told me this morning that I should keep my nose out of her affairs. I don't even know what that means."

"Maybe it doesn't mean anything," Tommy said.

"But she said 'affairs.' What else could she mean?"

"How would I know? But if it was, like, an *affair*, she wouldn't tell you about it, right? So it must be something else."

"I guess," Nicky said. "But what?"

Chapter
10

It was the day of the Snow Ball. Nicky woke up excited, and nervous. He had dreamed the night before about dancing—about being at the Snow Ball, in front of Amy and Donna and Dirk Van Allen, and really dancing. He had flown around the dance floor. The people had stopped and stared—and applauded.

When he woke up, though, he felt like his clumsy old self. He went downstairs.

His mother was drinking coffee with Uncle Frankie while Grandma Tutti cooked something on the stove. His uncle cleared his throat and said, "Yo, Nicky D. How'd you sleep?"

"Okay," Nicky said. "What are you guys doing?"

"Nothing," Frankie said. "What does it look like?"

Nicky said, "It looks like you've got some kind of secret."

Frankie and Nicky's mother looked at each other.

"Us? *Fugheddaboudit*," Frankie said. "We're just talking. Pour me another cup of coffee, will you?"

Tommy came down a few minutes later, rubbing his eyes and grinning. The grown-ups got busy with their plans for the day and left the two boys to their breakfast and their own schemes. Grandma Tutti hovered around them, pouring juice, washing plates and humming to herself.

Once they'd eaten, Nicky took Tommy into the den and said, "What are we going to do today?"

Tommy thought about that. "Shouldn't we stay here and wait to see what that reporter comes up with?"

"No," Nicky said. "If we sit here waiting for the phone to ring, I'll go nuts."

"You're already nuts," Tommy said. "But he's not going to figure anything out in just a day, right?"

"Right," Nicky said. "Especially on Sunday. Maybe you could help me with the dancing one more time, before tonight."

"You don't need any help," Tommy said. "You just need to dance. When the music is on, just go for it. You'll be fine."

"I'm nervous," Nicky said.

"That's okay," Tommy said. "Sometimes a little nervous is good. Keeps you on your toes. What are we doing in the meantime?"

"I don't know," Nicky said. "We could try to get Clarence to take us somewhere, like to Walter's dad's bookstore."

"Yeah," Tommy said. "I guess we could. . . ."

"Okay, that's not the best idea," Nicky said. "We could do laser tag again, or go to the movies."

Grandma Tutti came into the room, drying her hands on a towel. "Why are you inside? You should go out on a nice sunny day like this."

"Grandma, it's a nice freezing day."

"So put on your warm clothes and go do something freezing. Aren't you supposed to go skating on a lake or something, out here in the woods?"

"Skate on a lake?" Tommy laughed. "Get out of here."

"No, she's right," Nicky said. "There's ice-skating at Lake Brenner."

"Outside? On a real lake?"

"Sure," Nicky said. "All the kids go there. It's a real scene."

"Then let's make the scene," Tommy said.

An hour later, the boys were lacing up their skates in front of the rental booth at the lake. They were bundled up to their noses, in two pairs of wool socks, two pairs of pants, ski jackets, mufflers and wool caps, leaving nothing exposed but their eyes.

"How are we supposed to skate like this?" Tommy said. "I can hardly move."

"You'll get used to it," Nicky said.

* * *

Peter Van Allen had had a restless night—his first one in years. It reminded him of the old days. The *bad* old days, when he'd lived his life looking over his shoulder, wondering when his past would catch up with him.

It never had, until just then. He'd had a good run. He'd made a place for himself. And he'd done it all legally. That was the joke. He'd been a failure as a criminal, and a big success playing by the rules. And now it was all over.

He sat in his car outside his house the next morning, unshaven and red-eyed, with the heater running and the windows fogging up, trying to think.

O'Farrell wanted twenty-five thousand dollars for telling him the name of the guys who had figured out that he was Peter Arlen, and for keeping the story out of his newspaper.

The money didn't bother Van Allen—that was pocket change—but the blackmail did. If a guy knew you'd pay him to stay quiet, he was going to want to be paid again, to *keep* staying quiet. And again after that.

For now, he didn't have a choice. He couldn't afford to let anything get in the way of the Fairport deal. If he could keep O'Farrell quiet for another few days . . . Well, *then* he could get rid of him. Permanently.

That would mean several guys to get rid of—O'Farrell and the guys who knew he was Patrick Arlen.

That was a lot of guys to worry about. He couldn't think about all of them at once. First things first. He picked up his cell phone and dialed. He listened to an answering machine voice that said, "You've reached Sean O'Farrell at the *Ridgeway Register*. Please leave your message after the beep. Ta-ta for now."

"It's me," Van Allen said after the beep. "I have something for you. Call me back."

The ice stretched almost all the way down the long, thin lake, where, many summers before, Nicky had taken his first swimming lessons and later learned how to sail a small boat. Now it was white with cold and marked with shadows from the bare trees on its banks, and crowded with kids and families and groups of rowdy teenagers.

Nicky led Tommy to the ice and pointed to places in the distance that were closed off by bright yellow signs that said, DANGER. DO NOT ENTER.

"What're those?" Tommy asked.

"Thin ice," Nicky told him. "Whatever you do, don't go skating over there. People fall in and freeze to death."

"Wearing all these clothes? I don't think so."

"Just remember you're a beginner, and stay away from those parts," Nicky said. "You'll be okay."

"Whatever," Tommy said, and skated unsteadily onto the ice.

Within minutes, he was scooting around like a pro.

"I thought you said you'd never done this before," Nicky said.

"Only roller skates and in-line skates," Tommy said.

"You're good!" Nicky said just as Tommy lost his balance and fell onto the ice.

"Stop talking to me!" Tommy said.

The boys skated for an hour. Tommy got more and more comfortable on the ice and skated faster and faster. "Check this out!" he said, and skidded to a stop that sent ice showering over Nicky's head.

"You're not supposed to do that," Nicky said. "It leaves marks on the ice."

"Stop worrying," Tommy said. "You're always worrying about the rules and stuff. I'll race you to the end of the lake and back."

Nicky looked. It was probably an eighth of a mile to the end. Almost no one was skating down there. Even though the rules said you weren't supposed to speed skate, they could probably get away with it on the empty part of the ice.

"Okay," Nicky said. "But take it easy until we get to that second group of trees. Then no one will yell at us for skating fast."

The two boys kept pace until they were almost at the trees. Then Tommy said, "Go!" and took off.

Nicky was a good skater. It wasn't hard for him to keep up with Tommy. It wasn't hard for him to beat him, either. But he didn't want to make him feel bad, so he skated just about Tommy's speed until they neared the yellow warning signs at the end of the lake.

"Get offa me," Tommy yelled.

"No way," Nicky yelled back. "I'm going to beat you."

"No way to *that*," Tommy shouted.

Nicky called out, "Let's turn around. But watch your skates. This ice has been in the sun all day and it's slip—"

Tommy, trying to make the turn too fast, skidded on the ice. His skates went out from under him, and he fell hard on his backside. Then he slid on the ice, his legs and arms sprawling around him, until he was past the yellow warning signs. Nicky stopped.

"Tommy!" he called. "Don't move. Stay down."

"I'm okay," Tommy said, and got to his knees. "And I'm still going to beat you."

As he got to his feet, the ice around him made a terrible cracking sound. Nicky shouted, "Get down!" and dropped to his knees. Tommy remained standing. The ice around him shattered, and he slipped straight down into the icy water.

Nicky looked toward the parking lot and the skate-rental shack. Too far! No one could see them from there. When he looked back, Tommy had bobbed to the surface. He was sputtering and coughing and grabbing at the slick ice with his hands.

Nicky began crawling toward Tommy, who by then had gotten his hands on the ice and had stopped thrashing around. When Nicky was ten feet away, he lay flat on the ice and started scooting forward on his belly.

"I'm coming!" he said. "Try not to move too much, all right?"

Tommy tried to speak but couldn't.

Nicky was only six feet away. He could see cracks in

the ice between him and Tommy. He looked back toward the skate-rental shack. No one was coming.

Nicky took his muffler off and made it into a ball. Holding one end, he threw the ball at Tommy. The muffler stretched out and lay flat on the ice—but not close enough for Tommy to grab. Nicky scooted forward and tried again. Still not close enough. Nicky scooted forward a bit more. The ice groaned but didn't crack.

"This time it'll work," he said. "Ready?"

Tommy nodded. His face was getting blue.

Nicky balled up the muffler and threw it. Bull's-eye. Tommy took the muffler in one hand, and then in two. Nicky began to pull.

The ice began to groan and crack again when Tommy climbed onto it.

"Wait!" Nicky said, and scooted backward. "Now go."

Tommy pulled himself a little more onto the ice, which groaned and cracked again.

"Wait!" Nicky said, and scooted backward another foot.

Tommy was shivering violently when Nicky got him all the way onto the ice. He tried to speak, but his lips were too cold.

Nicky said, "It's okay. You're going to be okay. We have to skate back to the parking lot, and we've got to skate fast to get warm. Okay?"

Tommy nodded.

"Let's go."

The skate-rental men shouted at Nicky and Tommy for skating too close to the edge. Then they brought the boys into their shack and got Tommy out of his jacket and sweater and one pair of pants, then planted him in front of the heater while they called Nicky's mother to get the boys.

Tommy shivered all the way back to the house, where Nicky's mother put him in a warm bath and got Grandma Tutti to make him a mug of cocoa.

Sitting at his desk that morning, listening to his messages, O'Farrell rubbed his hands together and said, "You've done it, Sean, old boot. You've got the fish on the line."

The money would be very welcome. O'Farrell made next to nothing as a reporter. But he wasn't really a reporter anymore. He had been, back in the old days. Then he'd become a criminal. He still wrote stories for the newspaper, but he made his money doing favors for people like Patrick Arlen and Peter Van Allen—rich people who got into trouble and needed help getting out. O'Farrell knew how to get police records and destroy them. He knew how to buy protection from politicians. He knew how to get politicians elected. He knew how to get people killed.

Leaving the *Ridgeway Register* offices at midday, bundled up against the cold winter weather, O'Farrell felt a twinge. When he got his money, he was going to tell Patrick Arlen about the boys. What would Arlen do then?

The bad feeling stuck with him. He didn't like it.

Halfway down the block, O'Farrell turned and stepped through the door of the Snug Harbor. Inside, it was dark and smoky, and behind the bar were things that could make a man stop feeling bad.

O'Farrell sat on a stool and said, "Let's have a little of that Irish whiskey, Jim, and be quick about it."

Hours later, back at the house, Tommy's temperature was normal and he'd stopped shaking. Nicky's mother had wrapped him in a big bathrobe and given him cup after cup of hot cocoa. Sitting in the living room, swaddled like a newborn baby, he was having a hard time staying awake.

"You can't fall asleep," Nicky said. "We'll miss the Snow Ball."

"Stop worrying," Tommy said sleepily. "I'm fine."

Nicky's father and Uncle Frankie came in and listened as Nicky's mother told the story of Tommy's fall through the thin ice. Nicky's father was very upset.

"Nicholas knows better than to go anywhere near that end of the lake," he said. "This is very irresponsible behavior. Tommy could have drowned, or frozen to death!"

"Aw, give the guys a break," Frankie said. "It was an accident."

"Frankie, Tommy could have *died*. Both boys could have."

"Okay—but they didn't!" Frankie said.

"But they could have," Nicky's father said.

"What are you, Xena the Worrier Princess?" Frankie said. "You're angry about something that could have happened, instead of being happy about what didn't happen. Or instead of being proud of your son for being a hero. What he did on the ice was pretty brave."

It seemed Nicky's dad hadn't thought of that. He looked at Nicky, whose eyes had begun to fill with tears.

"You must have been scared," Nicky's father said.

"I was," Nicky said, and wiped his eyes. "I thought Tommy was going to die. I thought we *both* were. My hands were shaking and I was almost crying. I felt like such a coward."

Nicky hid his face in his hands.

"Whoa!" Frankie said. "Wait a minute! Why would you say that?"

Nicky looked up at him. "Because I was scared."

"Scared? That doesn't make you a coward," Frankie said. "That makes you a *hero*! Do you think being brave means not being afraid?"

Nicky wiped his nose on his sleeve. "Well, yeah."

"That's not it at all!" his uncle said. "Anybody can do something scary when he's not scared. But it takes a hero to do something scary when he knows he's in danger. *That's* bravery. A coward would have left his friend on the ice and run away. Only the brave guy stays behind and tries to help—especially when he knows he's about to fall in, too."

"So . . . you get scared, sometimes?"

"I get scared *all* the time," Frankie said. "It comes with the job. Doing the right thing even when you're scared— that's what it's all about."

"All right, then," Nicky's father said. "Nicky gets the bravery medal for saving his friend. And the honesty medal for telling his parents the truth about what happened. And the stupid medal for going onto the thin ice in the first place. Fair enough?"

Tommy said, "I think I'm the one who gets the *stupid* medal. The others are for Nicky."

"You can share them all," Nicky's father said. "Now I'm going to make myself a drink. Frank, how do you take your whiskey?"

"In a glass," Frankie said. "But I'm gonna say no for right now. I gotta get back to Brooklyn and pick up Donna, remember? So your son will have a date for this Snow Ball thing."

It was late afternoon before Van Allen got the call. He checked his watch and said into the cell phone, "I can be there in half an hour."

The Snug Harbor sounded like the perfect place—a crummy bar in downtown Ridgeway. No one would know him there. Nice people like Peter Van Allen didn't go to places like that.

O'Farrell was waiting when he arrived, sitting with a pipe in his mouth and smoke swirling around his curly blond hair. He looked up and winked at Van Allen but said nothing. Van Allen slid onto the barstool next to him and said to the bartender, "Vodka martini. Dry."

Van Allen watched the man pour his drink, and slid a brown paper package out of his jacket pocket onto

O'Farrell's lap. The Irishman took the money without a word and put it into his own jacket.

"Thanks," Van Allen said as the bartender set his drink on the bar and walked away. Then, without looking at O'Farrell, he said, "Okay. Give."

"His name's Nick, or Nicky," O'Farrell said. "And he's got a friend, a tough-looking lad who sounds like he's from Brooklyn."

Van Allen turned to O'Farrell and said, "And?"

"And nothing," the Irishman said. "That's it."

"*What?* Twenty-five grand for *'Nick'*?"

"If I'd known his last name, my friend, I'd have asked for fifty—and you'd have paid." O'Farrell got to his feet and leaned close to Van Allen. "Ta-ta for now. And good luck."

Van Allen gulped his martini and asked for another. Nick? *Nicky?* He tried to stay calm, and to think. Had he ever known a guy named Nick?

There was Nick the Nose, with the big sneezer, but he was from Atlantic City, and he was dead. There was Nicky Noodles, who never ate anything but pasta, but he was from Buffalo, and he was in prison. There was Nick the Nap, who always fell asleep in class, but that was almost forty years ago, in second grade. Nick the Nap had grown up to be a dentist.

Van Allen didn't know any other Nick, with or without a friend from Brooklyn.

What *was* this? Was he being hustled? Maybe O'Farrell had made the whole thing up. Of course! How could he have been so stupid?

He never should have gotten involved with O'Farrell in the first place. But he'd needed help. When he'd stopped being Patrick Arlen and reinvented himself as Peter Van Allen, he had needed someone to destroy his police files in Ridgeway. He couldn't ask a cop. So he looked for the next best thing—someone who knew the story and was friendly with the cops. He found O'Farrell . . .

. . . who was now double-crossing him. What a rat! What a world! You couldn't trust *anyone*, not even your own partner—a lesson that poor old Nicholas Borelli was about to learn with the Fairport deal. Come Monday, when they got to the bank and Borelli saw the actual paperwork . . .

Well, that wasn't Van Allen's problem. Borelli, the sap, had been foolish enough to trust him, and now he was going to pay the price. Too bad, in some ways. Nicholas Borelli was a pretty good guy. Nick Borelli was the kind of guy who—

Nick Borelli! *Nick!* Van Allen choked on his drink. It was Borelli!

O'Farrell had said "Nick" and a friend who sounded like he was from Brooklyn. Borelli's brother was from Brooklyn! And he was a cop!

Holy cow! It had been right under his nose the whole time! Van Allen slid a twenty-dollar bill onto the bar and went outside. It was just getting dark. But inside his head, it was very bright—bright and hot and angry. He'd fix that Borelli. *And* his little brother from Brooklyn.

* * *

By dinnertime, Tommy had fallen asleep in the den. They didn't wake him. Nicky's mother wanted to. But Grandma Tutti said no.

"You know the saying. Let the lying dog sleep," she said. "I'll warm up leftovers when he wakes up. Now sit, everybody."

It was another gigantic meal—minestrone soup with a loaf of fresh bread, followed by ravioli in a meat sauce, followed by braciole with broccoli rabe, roast potatoes and grilled fennel. And a ricotta pie for dessert.

"That was a great meal, Ma," Nicky's father said. "You're spoiling me rotten. What will I do when you're gone?"

"Now stop!" Nicky's mother said. "I've had enough of this. You've all been making fun of my cooking ever since your mother arrived, and I'm tired of it. I've put healthy food on this table for years and years, and I don't remember anyone saying a *word* about it until she got here. I'm sorry you don't appreciate what I'm trying to do for you. If you want unhealthy food, you can cook your own meals from now on."

"Now wait a minute," Nicky's father said.

"No," Nicky's mother said. "I don't want to hear another word about it—except 'I'm sorry.'"

"You're right," Nicky's father said. "And I'm sorry." He got up and put his hands on Nicky's mother's shoulders. "You are a wonderful cook. A loving cook. I guess I never realized how seriously you took the health thing. I thought it was just, you know, like, that you wanted to stay thin, or that it was, I don't know, *trendy* to be vegetarian."

"But I—"

"Stop!" Grandma Tutti told Nicky's father. "You're making it worse. 'I'm sorry' was a beautiful thing to say. After that, not so beautiful. I'll go make coffee."

Nicky's mother got up from the table and wiped her eyes. "You boys go into the den. I'll help Tutti serve the ricotta pie."

Nicky and his father sat with their feet up, waiting for their coffee and dessert. Tommy, lying on the sofa, snored quietly.

Nicky's father said, "You know, you probably saved his life today."

"I know," Nicky said.

"Now he's your responsibility forever."

Bringing in the coffee cups and dessert plates, Nicky's mother said, "It's almost time for you to get ready for the ball. What are you going to do about Tommy?"

Nicky looked at his watch and said, "I don't know. He'll hate me if I go without him."

"Go without me where?" Tommy said. He sat up on the sofa, blinking at the room.

"We're talking about the Snow Ball," Nicky's mother said. "But you probably don't feel much like going."

"Who, me?" Tommy laughed. "You don't think I'd miss the Snow Ball just because of a little dip in the lake."

"I don't know," Nicky's mother said.

"Aw, I'm fine!" Tommy said, and jumped to his feet. "Look!"

"His temperature was normal," Grandma Tutti said.

"Please?" Nicky asked.

Everyone turned to Nicky's father. His face was stern. He turned to Nicky's mother and said, "What do you think? Should we make him stay home?"

"What do *you* think?"

Nicky's father smiled. "Go get dressed. Clarence will drive you over."

"Yes!" Nicky said. "Thanks."

"Your uncle Frankie will show up at some point with Donna," Nicky's father added. "Your mother and I will stop by later. Have fun."

"Come on!" Nicky said. "Let's get ready."

Chapter
11

The Carrington Country Club was decked out for the Snow Ball. The long sloping drive and the outside of the reception hall were strung with lights. The inside had been decorated to look like an igloo. Men and women in white fur-lined parkas welcomed the visitors to the ball, taking their coats and overshoes and leading them to the main ballroom.

It, too, was a winter wonderland. The ceiling was hung with "icicles." The walls were banked with "snow." Roaring fires burned in the huge stone fireplaces at each end of the ballroom. The air smelled of woodsmoke and pine. Soft rock music played—the Eagles? Or was it Fleetwood Mac? It was the kind of stuff Nicky had heard on his parents' '70s and '80s compilation CDs. The dance floor was already half filled with couples, most of them Carrington parents, dancing cheek to cheek.

"Wow," Tommy said. "Some layout. Where's the food?"

"We just ate!"

"I know, but we didn't have dessert."

"This way," Nicky said. "There's punch and cookies over there, I bet."

Chad and Noah were hogging the punch bowl. Jordan tugged on Nicky's necktie and said, "What is that—curtains?"

"It's paisley," Nicky said, straightening his tie.

"You look like furniture."

Chad told Tommy he knew about Nicky's dance lessons and wanted some for himself. Noah told Tommy he was already a great dancer and didn't need any lessons.

"Who asked you?" Tommy said. "So go dance."

When Noah was gone, Nicky said, "You notice someone missing?"

"Like who?"

"Like Mr. Van Allen," Nicky said. "He's the club treasurer. He should be here."

"Maybe he's busy killing someone."

"Don't say that!" Nicky said.

"Maybe it's Dirk," Tommy said.

"Don't say that, even."

"I'm only kidding," Tommy said. "Pour me some punch."

The ballroom began to fill up. Nicky introduced Tommy

to some more of his school friends. One of them said, "You're the guy who knocked out Dirk Van Allen!"

"Not me," Tommy said. "I roughed him up some, but—"

"I heard you broke his nose," another kid said.

"Well," Tommy said, "I might've bruised it a little."

"That's enough, bruiser," Nicky said. "Look who's here."

Tommy turned. Marian and Amy Galloway had just entered the ballroom, tall and elegant, like a queen and her princess daughter.

"Wow," Tommy said.

"You got that right," Nicky said. "Wow."

The two Galloways walked directly toward Nicky and Tommy.

"Good evening, boys," Marian Galloway said. "I don't think I see your parents here, Nicky. Or your uncle."

"Hello, Tommy," Amy said. "Hello, Nicky."

"Hi," Nicky said. "They're coming. My uncle is driving down from Brooklyn, with another friend of ours."

"Could that be Donna, that *friend?*" Amy asked.

Nicky began to blush. "Well, I . . ."

"I *thought* so," Amy said. "Is she bringing a friend for Tommy? I hate to think of him being all alone at the Snow Ball."

"Don't worry about me," Tommy said. "I'm with *you*. Let's dance."

Amy allowed herself to be escorted onto the dance floor.

"Brooklyn charm!" Marian Galloway said. "Who knew?"

A few minutes later, Nicky saw Uncle Frankie come into the ballroom. On one arm was Grandma Tutti. On the other was Donna.

To Nicky, she was a vision.

That made him shy. Donna seemed shy, too. Even though it had been only days since they had seen each other, Nicky felt funny saying hello to her.

"Hi."

"Hi."

"So, you made it."

"Yeah."

"Did you drive down with my uncle?"

"In a police car. Unmarked."

"Cool." Nicky couldn't think of what to say. "Suburban?"

"No," Donna said. "Crown Victoria."

"Cool."

The song ended. Tommy and Amy stopped dancing. Nicky's grandmother had noticed Father David across the room. She waved and excused herself, saying, "Nicky, don't get into trouble with all these girls here."

"Yeah, take it easy, you little heartbreaker," Tommy said. "Let's dance. Can you do something about the music?"

"Maybe," Nicky said. "See if the girls want some punch, and I'll find out."

"Ladies?" Tommy said, and offered Amy and Donna his arms. "This way."

Nicky found Walter Wager, the kid Tommy had saved

from Dirk Van Allen, working the music. "Hey," Nicky said. "They made you deejay?"

"Yeah," Walter said. "You haven't seen Dirk tonight, have you?"

"Maybe he's not coming," Nicky said. "Maybe he's ashamed of himself, acting like that at the mall."

"Yeah, sure—Dirk Van Allen, ashamed," Walter said. "That'll be the day."

"Well, he's not here now anyway," Nicky said. "Since you're doing the music, could you put on something different? Like, something actually recorded in our lifetime?"

Walter grinned and said, "Oh, *yeah*."

Young people got up all over the ballroom when the new music started. Kids were jumping and hopping. Nicky found Tommy already on the dance floor with Amy and Donna. Tommy winked at him and said, "Go, dude."

Nicky began to dance. He tried to remember the moves Tommy had shown him. There was the one where you twisted from side to side. There was the one where you pumped your arms back and forth, in and out. He tried to remember to pick up his feet a little. It felt very unnatural. He smiled at Donna and tried to look relaxed.

At the end of the first song, Tommy took his arm and said, "What are you *doing*?"

"I don't know. Just dancing."

"That's not dancing. What's the problem?"

"I'm just trying to be careful and not make any mistakes."

"Well, stop," Tommy said. "Being careful is the worst

thing you can do. You have to lay it out there, see? You have to go for it. If you're going to dance, you have to *dance*. If you try to look good, too, you're going to look like an idiot."

The next time, Nicky cut it loose. He went all out. He closed his eyes and listened to the beat and let his body move. And it felt *great*. Did he look like an idiot? He didn't care.

"Yeah!" Tommy said. "That's what I'm talking about."

"Yeah!" Nicky said back at him.

"Woo-hooo," Donna yelled.

Nicky, pleased with himself, closed his eyes and let himself go.

Peter Van Allen dropped Mrs. Van Allen and Dirk at the front doors of the Carrington Country Club. He gave his wife a peck on the cheek and said, "I'll be along just as soon as I take care of this piece of business. If I'm running late, make my apologies, won't you, dear? Tell them to go on without me."

"But, Peter! What will people—"

"Just do it!" he barked. "I mean, please. Just—cover for me."

Van Allen pulled his car into the club parking lot and shut off the engine. Then he pounded the steering wheel and said, "Damn! Damn! Damn! *Why?* Why did this have to happen? And why *now?* One more day to get everything signed, and now *this!*"

He had to *think*. He couldn't let that Borelli outsmart

him. The double-crosser! He had probably been planning this all along. Italians!

Van Allen looked at his watch. Nine o'clock. In thirteen hours, the bank, the notary public and the escrow company would be open. If he didn't have Borelli there, and the papers weren't signed, the whole thing would be lost. And if Borelli knew who he was and went public with it, Van Allen would go to prison.

Well, Peter Van Allen was not going to prison. Patrick Arlen was *definitely* not going to prison.

He leaned over and opened the glove compartment. Inside, wrapped in black cloth, was a shiny black Beretta 9 mm handgun. Van Allen tucked the weapon into his waistband and closed the glove compartment. He let out a laugh and started the car.

After three more songs, the music stopped and Stanley Smoot, the president of the Carrington Country Club, spoke to the dancers through a microphone.

"Good evening, ladies and gentlemen, and thank you for joining me tonight for this Seventy-third annual Snow Ball," he said. "I'm delighted to see all you young people here, too, and to see so many of you already enjoying this fine music. Like you kids say, it's *hell-o* good. Heh-heh."

There was no laughter. Smoot continued without interruption.

"As you all know, the Snow Ball dance committee presents prizes to the best dancers—best individual dancer, best dance couple, and best slow-dance couple. Our judges are already on the floor, making notes. The names of the winners will be announced by our own treasurer, Mr. Peter Van Allen, at eleven o'clock, and the winners will receive their prizes—generously donated, I might add, by Carrington Clock and Watch, and by the Village Hobby Shop. I wish you all good luck, and 'dance, dance, dance'!"

"Do you have to live around here to win?" Tommy asked. " 'Cause otherwise it's in the bag."

"I wouldn't get too cocky," Amy said. "Now that Nicky's such a good dancer . . ."

"I taught him everything he knows!"

"Come teach *me*, then," Amy said.

The music started again. Nicky, self-conscious now that he knew judges were watching, pulled Donna onto the floor and began to move around carefully.

"You're doing it again!" Tommy yelled at him.

"Doing what?"

"Dancing like you got Jell-O in your pants. Relax!"

The next song was slow. Donna took Nicky's hand and said, "I don't really know how to do this, but I bet you do."

"It's nothing," Nicky said. "Just follow me."

Across the room, Nicky saw his mother and father step onto the dance floor. He saw uncle Frankie and Marian Galloway near them. His uncle looked as graceful as a gorilla. Behind him, he saw Grandma Tutti dancing with some old geezer. It appeared to be Dr. Feldman—Carrington's only resident psychiatrist.

Nicky was wondering what in the world his grandmother and a psychiatrist would talk about when he felt a tap on his shoulder. Passing close to him were Tommy and Amy, dancing nicely.

"Look at me! Doing the box step!" Tommy said. "I'm gonna win the slow-dance prize, too."

"Go for it," Nicky said.

The songs alternated slow and fast. Nicky saw a judge making notes. Looking around, he realized he couldn't possibly win. There were too many dancers, and too many of them were good dancers—smooth, light on their feet, polished. Nicky decided to forget about the prizes, and the judges, and the other dancers, and just try to have a good time.

For the next song he was free and abandoned. He grinned at Donna. He felt the music. He *danced*.

When the song ended, there was another tap on his shoulder. Nicky said, "Tommy! Can't you leave me alone for five minutes?"

"No, I can't, Nicholas. I can't live a moment without you."

Nicky turned and stared. There was Dirk Van Allen, wearing a sports coat over a pair of low-slung rapper jeans.

"Dirk! What are you— Where's your dad?"

"Shut up, Borelli," Dirk said. "I'm here for your little friend. It's payback time."

"Forget it, Dirk, unless you want him to beat you up again."

"Not quite, squirt," Dirk said. "This time it's *me* that's going to beat *him* up."

152

Tommy was over by the punch bowl, standing with Uncle Frankie, Grandma Tutti and Nicky's parents. Tommy saw Dirk facing off with Nicky and said, "Uh-oh. That monkey Dirk is back again."

"That's okay," Frankie said.

"It's not," Tommy said. "Nicky's gonna need some help."

"No," Frankie said, taking Tommy's arm and holding him back. "Let him settle it himself."

"But listen," Tommy said. "The kid's dad—"

"That's the bully from school?" Tutti asked. "Nicky's no match for a boy like that."

"That's enough, Ma," Nicky's father said. "Let's leave Nicky alone."

"But Dirk's bigger than him, and he fights dirty," Tommy said. "Besides, there's—"

"Nicky needs to settle this now, by himself," Frankie said. "Nicky has to live here. You don't. Let him sort it out."

Dirk had already pushed Nicky in the chest once. Now he pushed him again.

"But maybe before I take care of Tommy, I should take care of you," Dirk said. "Because I'm sick of you. I've been sick of you since kindy-garten. Little Nicholas with the perfect grades. Little Nicholas, the teacher's pet. Look at you! You're nothing but a . . . a . . . a little nerd!"

Dirk pushed Nicky in the chest again. This time Nicky pushed back. Dirk stumbled and fell.

"Hey! Are you crazy?" Dirk said. "Why did you do that?"

153

"I'm tired of you pushing me around, Dirk," Nicky said. "I don't like it."

Dirk grinned. "Get used to it, Borelli. 'Cause I'm just getting started."

He struggled to his feet, holding up his baggy gangsta pants with one hand. Suddenly, to Nicky, he was a joke. Nicky saw the big bully in a way he'd never seen him before.

So he laughed at him. "You pathetic, pea-brained primate! Do you really think anyone is going to let you fight me here, at the Snow Ball? All you'll do is get us both in trouble."

"Okay, then," Dirk said. "Come outside and fight like a man. Unless you're chicken."

Nicky blushed. Now it was less funny. A crowd had gathered. Nicky could feel everyone staring at him.

"I'm not a chicken," he said. "I'm not any kind of animal. And I'm not going to fight you. Fighting is stupid."

"You're a chicken!" Dirk said, and began making chicken noises. "Puck-puck-puckety-puck. Here, chicky-chicky-chick."

"Let's see who's chicken," Nicky said. "Let's see if *you* are. If you think you're so tough, I'll challenge you right now to a dance-off."

"A *what?*"

"A dance-off. A dance competition. You and me. Two songs. We'll do it like follow-the-leader. I'll do a move. You copy it. If you can't do it, you lose."

"That's stupid!" Dirk said.

"Then you're the chicken," Nicky said.

Dirk raised his fists. "Take that back! And take back that thing about the primate! You think I don't know what those big words mean? Well, I *do*! Put 'em up!"

"Dirk Van Allen! Nicholas Borelli!" President Smoot stood staring at them. "Put your hands down at once. What's going on here?"

"Dirk wanted to fight," Nicky said. "I challenged him to a dance-off instead."

"There won't be any fighting here," Smoot said. "Whatever the problem is, you can settle it some other way."

Nicky and Dirk stared at each other. Dirk said, "Let me get this straight. It's a dance-off with *you*, not your little friend, right?"

"That's right," Nicky said. "With me."

Dirk looked at his friends, at Nicky, at Tommy and then at the ground. His face began to redden, and his fists balled up again.

"Dance!" someone in the crowd called out. "Dance!"

Other voices joined in. Soon it was a chant. "Dance! Dance! Dance! Dance!"

Dirk turned to Nicky. "Okay, little nerd man," he said. "Let's boogie."

Van Allen dialed Borelli's cell phone number from the car. When he answered, Van Allen said, "Hey, it's me. Listen, something has come up. Something urgent. I need to see you right away. I'm waiting for you at the clubhouse side entrance—*now*. Come quick. And come alone."

Van Allen hung up, dashed from his car to the side of

155

the country club building and stood in the shadows. Shivering in the dark, he figured he had a fifty-fifty shot. Borelli might know that Peter Van Allen and Patrick Arlen were the same guy, but Borelli didn't know that Van Allen *knew* he knew. So Van Allen had a little edge. If he used it right . . .

Nicky's father put his cell phone back into his pocket and turned to his wife. "I have to step outside for a minute," he said. "It's Van Allen. Something has come up."

"But Nicky is about to—"

"I'll be right back."

He went out the front door of the clubhouse and around the side of the building. He was a little nervous. Could something have gone wrong? Had Van Allen changed his mind? He checked his watch. In less than thirteen hours, the bank would be open and this would all be over. If he could only hold on to Van Allen for thirteen hours . . .

He found Van Allen at the side entrance.

"Hey!" Van Allen said. "I'm sorry to drag you away from the party. But something has come up. Do you have a car here?"

"Of course."

"We'll need it to run a quick errand. Do you have the keys?"

"Sure."

"Let's take a drive, then. It'll just take five minutes."

They walked together to the parking lot and got into the Navigator. Nicky's father started the engine.

"You like these big guys, huh?" Van Allen said.

"I never drive it," Nicky's father said. "It's the car my driver uses. But tonight, with all the kids, and my brother, and my mom . . ."

"Sure, sure," Van Allen said. "I get it. You got a lot of people depending on you."

"I'm a lucky man," Nicky's father said. "I got a great family."

"Sure you do," Van Allen said. "And if you ever want to see them again, you'll do exactly what I tell you to do. Get me?"

Nicky's father turned to stare at Van Allen, who was now aiming a nasty-looking gun at him.

"What the—"

"That's right, it's a gun," Van Allen said. "Now shut up and drive, and I won't have to use it. We're going to Fairport."

A team of judges—three adults and three kids—was assembled. One of the kids was Walter.

"That's not fair," Dirk said. "You can't use *Walter*."

"If we're not allowed to choose kids you've picked on, we'll be here all night," Nicky said. "Are you backing out?"

"No," Dirk said. "Start the music."

Nicky started off slowly—a little move, a little spin. Dirk was a clumsy dancer, but he had no trouble keeping up. Then the music changed. Nicky decided to go for it. He shook his arms and swung his feet. Dirk looked lost but tried to copy him. So Nicky fired it up all the way. He clapped his hands and spun around and shot his arms into the air. Someone in the crowd said, "Yeah! Go!"

Dirk was getting really lost. Nicky felt confident. He also felt the song coming to a close. When the last verse began, he closed his eyes, spun, turned, shot his arms into the air again and went down *hard* into the splits—just as he'd seen Clarence do.

The crowd roared and clapped. Dirk stared. He spun around, waved his arms idiotically in the air and fell onto the floor with a crash. There was a terrible ripping sound. His baggy pants split right up the middle.

Dirk stood up, grabbed his trousers in two hands and went running, red-faced, for the exit.

The music ended. The judges reached their verdict. It was Nicholas Borelli, five votes to one.

Walter pumped his fist in the air, then very quietly said, *"Yes!"*

Nicky, breathing hard, said, "Five to one? Someone voted *against* me?"

"Don't be greedy," Tommy said. "You won! Let's get something to drink."

Twenty minutes later, Stanley Smoot took the microphone. "May I have your attention, please? It's time to present the awards for the best dancers. Our judges have made their decisions. It is a tradition here at the

Carrington Country Club to have the prizes awarded by the club treasurer. But Mr. Van Allen seems to have been delayed."

Nicky stared at Tommy. "Is that bad?" he asked.

"Who knows?" Tommy answered.

"So I will make the presentations myself," Smoot continued. "The first award, for best slow-dance couple, goes once again to last year's winners, Mr. and Mrs. David Marsh. Dave! Edna! Come on up!"

That was no surprise. Mr. and Mrs. Marsh were amateur ballroom dancers. They won every year.

"Our second award, for best dance couple, goes to Dr. and Mrs. John Cunningham. John and Carol? Come on up here."

"It's fixed," Tommy said. "I didn't even see them."

"They're good dancers," Nicky said. "They won a couple of years ago, too."

"Our final award, for best individual, well—this is a first!" Smoot said. "This has never happened before, but the contest for best individual dancer has ended in a tie, between Nicholas Borelli the Second and a young man whose name no one seems to know. He's Nicholas' friend from Brooklyn. Boys, come up and claim your prizes!"

Nicky and Tommy ran forward, deafened by the applause, Nicky as red as an apple.

They shook Smoot's hand and accepted their prize envelopes. Tommy whispered to Nicky, "What's in here? Whatta we get?"

"Don't be greedy," Nicky said. "You won!"

He turned around to show the envelope to Donna and the others.

"Hey," he said. "Where's my dad?"

"So I'm wise to the whole thing," Van Allen said. "Despite your little plan—whatever it was—you lose. You thought you could fool me? You can't."

Borelli wanted to shout at him. He wanted to say, "Fool you? What plan? Turn me loose, you maniac!"

But he couldn't. Van Allen had forced him to drive the snowy streets to Fairport with the gun trained on him the entire time. He made him park outside the old brewery building. He pulled a roll of duct tape out of his pocket and bound Borelli's hands together. Then he stuck a strip of it across his mouth.

"The reporter you contacted? I own that guy," Van Allen said. "He warned me—a guy named Nick and his friend from Brooklyn. *That* was hard to figure out."

"Mmmmff."

"Sure, sure. Yell your head off. First thing in the morning, we're going in and signing all the papers. But now the name on the check is going to be *yours*, not mine. You're paying for the whole thing. But I'm going to own it. Squawk, and you'll get it. Go to the cops, and I'll come after that sweet family of yours. Get me?"

"Mmmmfff!"

"Yeah, yeah, whatever," Van Allen said. "You might as

well shut up. We got a few hours to go before the bank opens."

The Snow Ball was over. Outside, it had begun to snow again. Nicky's mother, his grandmother, Uncle Frankie and Donna stood outside the country club doors, waving goodbye to people and watching the snow fall.

Marian Galloway and Amy pulled up in the Galloway Mercedes. The driver's-side window came down slowly, and Mrs. Galloway's face smiled out.

"Thank you for a lovely evening, Francis," she said. "If you'd like to stop by for a nightcap, I'm going to be up for a while."

"Yeah, maybe later," Frankie said. "I'll stop by. Or I'll call."

"Good ni-ight," she said, and drove away.

"Francis?" Nicky's mother said. "Your brother is going to *die*."

"He is if he kids me about it," Frankie said. " 'Cause I'll kill him."

"I think it's *darling*," Nicky's mother said. *"Francis."*

"It's my real name, like Francis Albert," Frankie said.

Nicky's mother stared at him.

"Francis Albert Sinatra?" Frankie asked. "The singer? Didn't your husband teach you anything?"

"I'll ask him when I see him," Nicky's mother said. "If we ever find him."

After a moment, Nicky and Tommy jogged up from opposite directions.

"He's not here," Tommy said. "I checked inside and out."

"And I checked the parking lot," Nicky said. "The Navigator's gone."

"But it makes no sense," Nicky's mother said. "He wouldn't just *leave*."

"Maybe there's something else going on," Frankie said. "Did he say anything at all about where he was going?"

"Nothing!" Nicky's mother said. "He just said, 'Something has come up.' With Van Allen."

Nicky and Tommy looked at each other. Tommy stared at the ground.

Uncle Frankie caught that and said, "Okay—what?"

"We—that is, I—there's something we have to tell you," Nicky said. "Me and Tommy— Van Allen's a crook! He's not even Van Allen. He's Arlen! Patrick Van Arlen! Wait! Without the 'Van' part. Just Arlen. He murdered Arlen! And he's planning to trick Dad! He's—"

"Stop!" Frankie said. "What are you talking about? Start over."

Nicky told Frankie about overhearing Van Allen and the two thugs in the amusement park, then going to the library, then meeting Sean O'Farrell at the *Ridgeway Register*.

"And what were you planning to do about this?" Frankie asked. "Turn into Sherlock Holmes? Solve the whole thing without telling anyone?"

"We just found out!" Nicky said. "We were trying to

162

figure out what to do. We didn't want to get Dad in trouble. And we were scared."

"All right, all right, enough," Frankie said. "However it started, it don't look good now. It sounds like maybe Van Allen thought your dad was on to him. Could someone have told Van Allen? Who else knew?"

"Nobody," Nicky said. "I mean, us. And Van Allen, of course. And the reporter."

"And anybody they told, right?" Uncle Frankie said.

"But who would they tell?" Nicky's mother asked. "They're both in this up to their necks."

"Let's hope so," Frankie said. "And let's hope Nick's *not*. Do you know if there's anything illegal about the Fairport thing?"

"Of course there's not!" Nicky's mother said. "Remember who you're talking about."

"Then we've got a shot," Frankie said. He stared at the falling snow for a moment, then said, "Maybe we'll get lucky. Nicky, you got your cell phone?"

"Yes."

"Call the house. I'll call your father's cell. He ain't gonna be there, but we'll try."

For the next minute, everyone stood in silence while the phones rang. Nicky got the answering machine at home. Frankie got voice mail on the cell.

"All right . . . like I thought," Frankie said. "It's like this. We're all going to squeeze into the Crown Vic and go back to the house. Then I'm going to find my brother. Come on."

The ride home was quiet. The streets were empty. Cars parked along the road looked like great white beasts, slumped over asleep in the snow.

Frankie pulled into the Borellis' driveway and helped his mother, Nicky's mother and Donna get to the house. The sidewalk was slick with snow.

"I was planning on taking the lads back to the city," Frankie said. "That ain't gonna happen. Elizabeth, you gotta call Donna's folks and explain. But don't tell them what's going on. Just say it's late and I got a call and had to go to work. I'll run her home first thing tomorrow. And you gotta call Tommy's mom, too. Tell her the same thing."

"All right," Nicky's mother said. "But I'll have Tommy call and make his own excuses. Nicky, you're going to have to help me set up beds."

"No, he can't," Frankie said. "I need both of them with me. I don't know what this guy O'Farrell looks like. I don't know where Van Allen lives. And I don't know where the old brewery is. Guys, I need your help. A'right?"

"Is that where you think they are—at the brewery?" she asked.

"I don't know," Frankie said. "But it's one place to look."

Nicky's mother nodded grimly. "I know you'll be careful," she said. "But . . . you *will* be careful, won't you?"

"Nothing bad is gonna happen to nobody, I promise," Frankie said. "Except Van Allen. If he's got my brother, he's gonna wish he was never born."

Chapter 12

Frankie drove the Crown Vic across Carrington, following Nicky's directions, to the Van Allen estate. It was a big modern house right on the river. It looked deserted. The house lights were out. The porch lights were out. The front lawn and walkway were covered with an unbroken carpet of snow. There was no Navigator.

"They ain't here," Frankie said.

He drove to the interstate and headed south. There wasn't much traffic. The two boys sat in silence and watched the snowy streets go by.

"What's this do?" Tommy asked, pointing at the dashboard.

"That's the radio," Frankie said, and flicked it on. The car filled with the sounds of police business.

"Six-two-eleven in progress at Bay Twelve and Parkside," a dispatcher said. "Units in the vicinity respond."

"Possible one-eight at four-nine-oh Ramsgate," another dispatcher said. "Code black."

"Wow," Tommy said. "That's all police stuff? Is it in code?"

"Yeah, and it's all bad news," Frankie said. "Every one of those calls is someone in trouble. The six-two-eleven is armed robbery. The one-eight is a domestic violence shooting. Luckily that ain't our business tonight."

Frankie turned the dispatch radio off. Tommy tapped a small monitor on the dashboard and said, "How about this?"

"That's an onboard computer," Frankie said. "In case you need a readout on a suspect or something. You swipe the driver's license. Find out who's been naughty and who's been nice, just like Santa Claus."

"It's also a GPS, right?" Tommy said.

"Yeah," Frankie said. "You got MapQuest and all that. You can find anything."

"Nicky's dad has the same thing in his car," Tommy said.

"What, in the Navigator?"

"Yeah," Tommy said. "It's pretty cool. It was designed by the same guys that designed *BlackPlanet Two*, you know?"

"Technology, huh?" Frankie said. "What'll they think of next?"

A few miles on, he said, "Okay. Here's the Fairport exit. This brewery, is it right in downtown?"

"It's near the old boardwalk," Nicky said. "Down by the sea."

"Okay," Frankie said.

The Crown Vic slid along the darkened streets. Fairport was even more deserted than Carrington. Frankie drove into the historic downtown district. The busted-up brick buildings looked haunted.

"That's it, there," Nicky said, and pointed to the old brewery building. "That's Dad's building."

It looked like nobody had been around it for ages. The cars on the street were all buried in snow. The brewery doors looked undisturbed. Frankie idled the Crown Vic and looked at the empty streets.

"I think we struck out," he said. "Nobody's been around here tonight. Can you think of anyplace else they might be? Does Van Allen have a favorite bar or restaurant? Does he have a *goomada*?"

Nicky said, "A what?"

"A *goomada*," Tommy said. "A *goomar*. You know, a girlfriend on the side."

"How should *I* know?" Nicky said.

"Yeah, never mind," Frankie said. He turned the Crown Vic around and started toward the interstate. "We could look around all night for these guys. We're wasting our time."

"But what about the GPS?" Tommy said.

"What about it?" Frankie asked him. "Are we lost?"

"No, but we can use it to find the Navigator," Tommy said. "I read about it in a computer game magazine. These

167

guys in California use the GPS to play a giant game of hide-and-seek—like, all over a whole city. If they're all on the same GPS network, they can track each other. Alls you need is the system number."

"And how do you get that?"

"I think you need the license plate number and the password," Tommy said. "Pull over."

Tommy clicked on the GPS. He pushed Control and System. The screen read, *Enter coordinates*. Tommy said, "Okay, what's the plate number, Nicky?"

"It's, um—wait," Nicky said. "Oh-two-B-B-K-five-six-seven."

"Are you sure?" Frankie said. "How do you remember that?"

"Clarence calls the Navigator B. B. King, like the blues guy," Nicky said. "So it's B-B-K. Then it's five-six-seven in a row."

"Now the password," Tommy said. "It's gotta be six letters. What do you think?"

Frankie said, "It's not his middle name."

"I don't even know it," Nicky said.

"What about his nickname?"

"My dad? He doesn't have a nickname."

"Then what about yours?" Tommy said. He typed in "Nicky." The screen said, *Access denied*.

"That's not it," Frankie said. "That's five letters, anyway."

"Then what about this?" Tommy said. He typed in "NickyD," and the screen said, *Access granted*.

"Yes!" he said. "We're in."

The screen came up with a black background and a green map of the eastern United States. At one edge of the map were a single blinking red dot and a single blinking green dot.

"What're the dots?" Frankie asked.

"The green is us, and the red is them," Tommy said.

"Great," Frankie said. "Now we know we're both somewhere on the eastern seaboard."

"Wait," Tommy said. He hit the down-arrow key twice. The screen disappeared and came back with a different grid. That one showed the state of New Jersey.

"Okay," Frankie said, staring at the blinking red dot. "So we know they're not in Boston."

"Wait," Tommy said, and hit the down-arrow key twice more. The screen came back with a very tight grid—fifteen lines going left to right, fifteen going top to bottom. The blinking red dot and the blinking green dot were separated by two lines on the grid.

"They're here," Tommy said.

"Where?" Frankie said, and stared out at the dark streets.

"Like, two blocks that way, toward the water," Tommy said.

Frankie turned and stared at Tommy. "You're a genius, and you're wasting your life if you don't do something with that brain of yours," Frankie said.

Frankie turned the Crown Vic toward the sea and drove slowly. He turned at the next corner, and at the one after that.

They drove along the boardwalk, down the street where Nicky and Tommy had stopped for a hot chocolate on that freezing cold day when they'd overheard Van Allen and the two goons.

"Look," Nicky said. "There's that abandoned amusement park."

"And there's the Navigator," Frankie said. "Tommy, you're a genius. Let's drive by real slow and have a look."

Frankie drove the Crown Vic past the black Navigator, which was the only car on the street not covered in drifts of snow. As they passed, he and the boys stared at the car.

"Why are the windows like that?" Nicky asked.

"They're steamed up," Frankie said. "They must still be in there."

"And look," Tommy said. "There's no snow on the hood."

"The engine's running," Frankie said. "They must have the heater on, trying to stay warm."

"So what do we do?" Nicky asked.

"If it was anybody else, you'd call for backup," Frankie said. "For a situation like this, you'd get the SWAT team, a helicopter with floodlights, the whole deal."

"Cool!" Tommy said. "You're gonna call for the SWAT team?"

"No—not yet," Frankie said. He pulled the Crown Vic to the end of the block, swung around and parked on a side street. "See, I don't know what your dad is up to. If he's been doing something that's not kosher, I want him to have a lawyer handy before any more cops show up."

"So what do we do instead?"

"I don't know," Frankie said. "For now, we don't do nothing."

The snow began to fall again. Nicky and Tommy climbed into the backseat and stared out the rear window. After a while, Tommy slid down and curled up in the corner. "I keep thinking about falling in that lake, and I get sleepy all over again," he said. "Wake me up if something happens." Soon he was snoring.

Nicky continued to stare out the back window. He wasn't sleepy. He was scared. He couldn't stop thinking about his dad, stuck in that car with Peter Van Allen. Or with Patrick Arlen.

He said, "Do you think my dad's okay? I mean, Van Allen wouldn't do anything to him, right?"

"Van Allen needs him alive," Frankie said.

That made Nicky feel better. A little. He went back to staring at the Navigator across the dark street.

On Front Street, Van Allen had reclined the two front seats until they were almost flat. Then he'd slapped another piece of tape over Nicky's dad's eyes.

"There," he said. "Isn't that cozy? We can both get a little shut-eye so we're perky when the bank opens."

He lay back with the gun in his hand, closed his eyes and seemed to go right to sleep.

Nicky's father tried to breathe calmly and regularly. He

waited. He listened to Van Allen snore. He considered his options.

The car was running. He could slam it into gear and start driving. He'd crash, since he couldn't drive with his hands taped together and his eyes closed, but maybe . . . No. Van Allen would shoot him before they went ten feet.

Could he hit the door-unlock button with his elbow and try to roll out into the street? Sure. But Van Allen would shoot him before he got the door open.

He could lunge for the gun and grab it. But with what? His hands were bound, and he couldn't see anything, anyway. But if he shifted around in his seat and moved his feet, he could *kick* the gun away, if he could find it. Then he could . . .

"Settle down, you," Van Allen said, and snapped the gun up at him. "Stop moving around. If you wake me up again, I'll shoot you."

Nicky's father knew he wouldn't unless he had to. Van Allen needed to keep him alive until he could sign over the bank papers. *Then*, he thought. *He'll drive me someplace and shoot me then.*

Down the block, Frankie and Nicky watched the black Navigator. It was still and silent. Nothing moved. Nicky, glancing around the inside of the Crown Vic, said, "Hey, what's that red light on the dashboard?"

"We're probably overheating, from standing still," Frankie said.

"Then why's it say 'Fuel low' on it?"

Frankie turned and stared. "Oh, great. We're running out of gas."

"What's that mean?"

"It means we gotta turn the car off," Frankie said. "It's gonna get cold in here, fast, but we can't afford to be out of gas if they make a run for it. Sorry."

Frankie turned off the motor. The heater and the fan stopped. The air got colder at once. The windows began to steam up, too. Frankie mopped the glass with his sleeve, but it steamed over right away.

"This is bad," he said. "I don't want to, but I gotta call for backup."

Frankie pulled the radio off its hanger, clicked a button and said, "Alpha-six-two. Code in?"

There was silence. Then the radio crackled and said, "Roger, Alpha-six-two. Go ahead."

"Alpha-six-two requesting tactical assist, corner First and Front, township of Fairport, New Jersey. I need local help. Two SWATs, no paint, and a bird, holding."

Frankie held the radio and listened. Nicky said, "What was that?"

"I told 'em where we are, and what we need—two SWAT units, unmarked cars, and a helicopter, not over-head but waiting in the vicinity. If Van Allen moves, I want to be able to hit him fast. But I don't want him to know we're here until then."

The radio crackled again and said, "Roger that, Alpha-six-two. You're green. Stand by."

173

Frankie mopped the window with his sleeve again. The snow was coming down harder now. The streets had gone white. He could barely see the Navigator. *If they make a run for it now, I won't see them,* he thought. *I gotta do something, and quick.*

"This ain't good, Nicky," he said. "We're gonna have to force his hand. Can you drive a car?"

"No," Nicky said. "I don't know how."

"You're gonna have to learn quick. Here's what we're gonna do. I'm gonna fire this thing up and drive straight toward that Navigator. Right before we get there, I'm gonna slam the horn and turn on the lights. And right when we hit them, I'm gonna jump out of the car. You with me so far?"

Nicky gulped. "Yeah."

"Good. When I jump out, you're gonna slide across the seat, put the car in reverse and stamp on the gas. Just go straight back, and stop, and get down. Easy, right?"

Nicky gulped again. "I guess so," he said. He stared at the pedals under the dashboard. "The one on the right is the gas, right?"

"Oh boy," Frankie said. "This is gonna be interesting. C'mere."

Frankie started the Crown Victoria. He told Nicky to buckle his seat belt, then said, "What about Tommy?"

Nicky looked into the backseat. "He's still asleep."

"Let him sleep," Frankie said. "We got work to do."

Frankie pulled the Crown Vic down First Street, toward Front. He angled the car so that it was directly facing the side of the Navigator, which was about a half block away. Frankie took a deep breath, crossed himself and said, "Here goes nothing."

He mashed the gas pedal down. The Crown Vic shot forward. Frankie put one hand on the horn and the other on the lights. When they were ten feet from the Navigator, he said, "Now!" He blasted the horn, threw on the lights, swung the door open and leapt out.

The Crown Vic smashed into the side of the Navigator. Nicky was jerked forward. He slid across the seat, pulled the gearshift to R and stepped on the gas. The Crown Vic shot backward, skidding sideways on the snowy street, and went fifty feet before it sideswiped a parked car and ground to a stop. Tommy shouted, "What's going on?"

Van Allen didn't know what had hit them, but he didn't wait to find out. He shot up from his seat, opened the door and rolled out of the Navigator into a bank of snow. He heard a voice scream, "Freeze!" and laughed: *Freeze, in the snow.* Van Allen whipped his gun hand up and fired once in the direction of the voice. Then he got to his feet and started running.

Nicky's father had heard the horn, felt the blaze of lights, felt the Navigator lurch sideways as something huge smashed into it, and fallen over toward the passenger seat. He had felt the passenger door open and a rush of cold air come in as the Navigator bounced upright. He had heard a voice yell, "Freeze!" Then a shot had rung out.

That was all he needed to hear. He rolled toward the

open passenger door, fell out into a snowbank and struggled to his feet. He heard footsteps running to his left. He turned to his right and moved quickly away.

Frankie saw Van Allen, illuminated by the Crown Vic's headlights, then lost him as he dashed into the darkness. Frankie put his pistol down and started after him. He was headed for what appeared to be an abandoned amusement park, fenced off with chain link. Van Allen couldn't get far. Frankie, staying low, skidded along the snowy ground, hoping Van Allen couldn't see him any better than he could see Van Allen.

From across the street, Nicky saw the Navigator door fly open. The car's interior light came on. There was no one there!

His uncle crouched in front of the truck and shouted, "Freeze!" He had his pistol up, like he was about to shoot. Then Nicky saw his dad sit up in the driver's seat of the Navigator. He said, "Dad!" and jumped out of the Crown Vic. Suddenly Van Allen leapt out of the snow and fired in Uncle Frankie's direction, then dashed into the shadows.

Nicky ran to the Navigator and yanked the driver's-side door open. But his dad had disappeared. He stared into the back of the Navigator. Nothing!

Sirens split the night. Nicky jumped out of the Navigator. Two black Suburbans, with headlights blinking and sirens blaring, were rushing toward him. Their headlights suddenly shone on a man stumbling into the street, duct tape covering his mouth and eyes.

"Dad! Stop!" Nicky shouted. He ran to his father and shoved him off the street and into a deep snowbank—just as the two Suburbans skidded to a stop on the ice. Six men with guns leapt out of the big black trucks and said, "Police! Freeze!"

Nicky and his dad stuck their hands up as high as they would go.

Going across the snowy field, Frankie lost Van Allen and stopped at the chain-link fence. Gone! But wait—there was a break in the fence. Frankie slipped through and stared into the darkness ahead. There wasn't any moon. The lights from Front Street weren't very bright. Halfway into the amusement park it was pitch-dark.

But he could see Van Allen's footsteps in the snow. Moving slowly, Frankie followed them. A hundred feet on, the steps turned to the right and headed behind one of the rides. Frankie peered up through the dim light. He could make out a sign that said, HAUNTED HOUSE OF FUN.

Some fun! Frankie cursed and stumbled over the threshold onto a section of floor that shifted violently from left to right. He lurched to the side and slammed into the wall. Up ahead, he heard a crash. A voice said, "Damn it!"

Frankie hurried on. He felt his way around a dark corner. A few steps ahead, the floor turned into giant rollers.

Frankie's feet went out from under him and he fell onto the rollers. He said, "Damn it!" too, then put his hand over his mouth.

He heard footsteps running, ahead of him. Frankie hurried on in the dark.

"Van Allen!" he shouted. "This is Frankie Borelli. Quit while you can. I got backup coming. You stop now, we can talk. If I keep chasing you, it's gonna get ugly."

"Bring it on!" Van Allen yelled back. "You Mafia jerks don't scare me."

"I'm not the Mafia, you idiot!" Frankie shouted. "I'm the cops! Five minutes from now you're gonna have a SWAT team sitting on your head."

Van Allen laughed wildly. "Yeah, right, Borelli. All I see chasing me is one fat goomba. You make a nice target!"

Two shots rang out. Frankie hit the floor and waited. He heard footsteps running again. He got to his feet and crept forward.

Then he heard the helicopter and cursed under his breath. "Not yet!" he said. But suddenly the haunted house was as bright as day, as the helicopter swung its searchlight over the place. Frankie saw Van Allen, down a corridor, twenty feet ahead, surrounded by walls of glass. Van Allen saw him, too. He swung around and fired again. Glass shattered. Frankie dropped and lay flat on the floor.

The SWAT team got the duct tape off Nicky's dad's mouth and eyes. He told them what he could about Van Allen, Patrick Arlen and his kidnapping. And Frankie.

"He's a New York City police officer, undercover," he said.

"Is he armed?" a SWAT officer asked.

"I don't know," Nicky's dad said. "But the other guy is. Van Allen's got an automatic pistol."

"Let's move!" the SWAT officer said.

Tommy had jumped out of the Crown Vic behind Nicky. He helped Nicky get his dad on his feet and started with them toward the waiting Suburbans.

Nicky had tears in his eyes. He smeared them away with his shirtsleeve and turned to watch the SWAT team make their assault. They were heading for the main entrance to the amusement park.

"Look!" he said. "They'll never get in that way! Those gates are all locked."

"The place we got in—was it on the left or the right?" Tommy asked.

"The right," Nicky said. "But they'll never find it. We gotta help."

Tommy stared across the snowy street at the heavily armed SWAT team. He said, "Are you kidding? I'm not going over there."

"You stay, then," Nicky said. "I'll be right back."

"Nicky!" his father shouted. "Stop! *Stop!*"

Nicky heard. He disobeyed. He ran as fast as he could across the street, across the field and up to the chain-link fence.

He found the opening right away and slipped through. Then he heard gunshots. He called out, "Uncle Frankie!"

He forgot about the SWAT team and instead ran for the midway.

It was too dark to see anything. But suddenly the air was full of noise—the helicopter!—and a wide shaky beam of light dashed across the ground in front of him.

As the helicopter passed over him, the haunted house was illuminated. Nicky saw two figures inside, shimmering in walls of glass and mirror. Then one turned and fired, and the other dropped to the floor. Nicky saw broken glass rain over him. Then the helicopter turned, and everything went dark. Nicky dashed up the front steps of the haunted house and went into the hall of mirrors.

The helicopter swung around in the sky. Frankie cocked his head and listened. The bird would pass again and hit the amusement park with lights. He needed to be ready to take a shot this time. He could hear Van Allen's footsteps, somewhere ahead of him in the darkness. He moved forward, trying to get as close to Van Allen as possible before the light came up again.

The helicopter light swung across the midway, rushing toward the front of the haunted house. Frankie raised his weapon and got ready to fire. The helicopter engines roared. Then the light hit the haunted house. The hall of mirrors was as bright as day.

Frankie saw Van Allen and took aim—and then saw another Van Allen, and another, and another. He shifted his weapon, flashing from one target to the next. He saw Van Allen turn toward him and lift his gun. He flicked his weapon to the next Van Allen, then realized he was pointing at Nicky. He dropped his weapon just as Nicky screamed, "Frankie! Look out!"

The hall of mirrors was ablaze with light. Van Allen had twenty targets to choose from—nineteen reflections of Frankie standing with his gun. Van Allen picked one and fired. The target exploded into shards of glass. He picked two more, side by side, and fired again. The targets disappeared. He selected two more and fired twice in fast succession.

Bingo! Glass shattered and Frankie crumpled to his knees, then fell to the floor.

Nicky screamed, "No! Frankie! Uncle Frankie!"

The haunted house went black again as the helicopter passed. Van Allen turned and dashed down the hall of mirrors. He went around a corner, slowly feeling his way along in the darkness. There were walls in front of him and on two sides. *Dead end.* Van Allen turned and moved slowly back down the corridor.

Luckily the helicopter was coming around again. He waited. When the light hit the haunted house, he'd dash for the exit. He'd get back out to the street and make a run for it. With Borelli's brother out of the way, he had a shot.

The helicopter approached. Van Allen flexed his knees like a sprinter.

Light hit the haunted house like a sunrise. Nicky dashed to Frankie and fell to his knees beside his body, onto a pile of broken glass. He called, "Frankie!" but no one was there. He slid to the next mirror. No one. What the— "Uncle Frankie!"

Across the corridor, Frankie lifted his head and hissed, "Shut up, Nicky! And get down!"

Van Allen saw his chance coming. The helicopter was swinging around again. The wide circle of light was racing across the midway, toward the haunted house. When the floodlight swept over him, and he could see the whole corridor ahead of him, Van Allen shot forward—and slammed headfirst into the wall in front of him. He hit *hard* and fell dizzy to the floor. Glass showered over him.

Frankie was on his feet fast and got to Van Allen just as the light disappeared. He put his gun on Van Allen's head and said, "It's over. You're done. Drop your weapon."

It was two hours before they were all back at the Borelli house. Nicky's father had called Nicky's mother and Grandma Tutti on Frankie's cell phone. The backup units had carried Van Allen away. Another unit had been dispatched to arrest Sean O'Farrell. A tow truck had come with gas for the Crown Vic. The Navigator was dented but drivable. Frankie said to Nicky's father, "You okay to drive?"

"Sure," Nicky's father said. "As long as I don't have to drive alone. Nicky? Come with me? Tommy, you ride with Frank."

Nicky's mother cried when Nicky's father got home. So did Grandma Tutti. Ten minutes later, Amy and Marian Galloway were there—also crying.

"Jeez," Frankie said. "I'd hate to see what would have happened if I *hadn't* brought him back okay."

"Stop, you," Grandma Tutti said. "We're just crying happy, is all. We were frightened."

"You and me both," Frankie said. "And maybe the two Nickys, too. Not Tommy, though, right?"

"I was asleep in the car for most of it," Tommy said.

"That was the only safe place to be," Frankie said. "Nicky shoulda stayed there, too. But he had to be a hero. Again!"

Nicky blushed. "I didn't want to be a hero," he said. "I was afraid Van Allen was going to shoot you."

"And he did—about four times," Frankie said.

"But if he missed, why did you fall down?" Nicky asked. "I thought he killed you."

"That's what I wanted *him* to think," Frankie said. "I figured he had a lot of bullets, and if he kept shooting at my reflection, sooner or later he was going to shoot *me*. So I let him think he got lucky on the fourth or fifth shot. Otherwise, he woulda kept going until he hit me."

"Then he would've come back for me, I guess," Nicky's father said.

"I never trusted him," Grandma Tutti said. "I told you from the beginning he was no good."

"Ma! You never said a word."

"Well, I *thought* about it," Grandma Tutti said. "I told myself he was no good. But did you listen? No."

"Well, it's over," Frankie said.

"What'll happen to Mr. Van Allen?" Nicky asked.

"Van Allen's going to prison," Frankie said. "They can't lock you up for killing yourself, or even faking your own death, but they'll think up some other stuff for him—like fraud, kidnapping, assault, you name it. He's gonna be gone awhile."

"So what'll happen to Dirk?"

Frankie looked at Nicky for a moment. "He's gonna be around, and he's gonna have a hard time. That ain't nice, having a dad in prison. You're gonna want to cut him some slack." Nicky nodded.

"And you . . . you're gonna want to find a new business partner," Frankie told Nicky's father. "Maybe one who's not a crook. Not for nothing, but . . . you might ask my advice every once in a while. I do know a few people, you know."

"I knew it!" Grandma Tutti said. "You boys are going into business together!"

"Ma! I told you once already . . ." Frankie said. "Ah, whatever. For tonight, I'm not doing nothin'. I'm beat. I'm gonna get some sleep before it's tomorrow already."

"It's tomorrow already *already*," Grandma Tutti said. "It's five o'clock in the morning."

"That's late enough for me," Frankie said. "I'll see you all tomorrow. Or today. Or whatever. Good night."

"Me too," Nicky's dad said. "I'm all in. Marian? Maybe you and Amy could come back for breakfast, and the boys can tell you the whole story then."

"Fine," Mrs. Galloway said. "We'll come back at, say, ten?"

"Eleven," Nicky's mother said. "Let's call it brunch."

"Brunch!" Grandma Tutti said. "I'm going back to bed, too. But I'm not eating anything called brunch. I'll make eggs and sausages. You can call it what you want."

"Nicky?" his mother said. "Do you think you could sleep a little?"

"No," he answered. "No possible way."

She smiled. "I didn't think so. Why don't you boys make yourself some cocoa and try to relax? Maybe you can get a little nap in front of the TV."

When all the grown-ups had gone to bed, Nicky and Tommy took their hot chocolate into the den and turned on the big-screen TV. There were highlights from some kind of winter sports competition. Boys on snowboards, dressed in baggy pants and parkas and goggles, were shooting up the sides of half-pipes and doing crazy spins in the air.

"You think you could do that?" Tommy asked Nicky.

"No," Nicky said. "Like, never."

"I could," Tommy said. "A week of practice, or two. I could do that."

"Have you ever been on a snowboard?"

"No, but it looks just like skateboarding," Tommy said. "How hard could it be?"

Nicky laughed.

"Listen," Tommy said. "I'm sorry about bailing out on you at the amusement park back there."

"Forget about it," Nicky said. "I mean, *fugheddaboudit*."

"I was scared."

"So was I," Nicky said. "I was scared to death."

"But you went in."

"I was scared to death."

The boys were quiet then. Nicky turned down the sound on the TV. The snowboarders slipped and slid and spun through the air. Nicky suddenly felt tired—dead tired. He set his cocoa down and sat back in the sofa. What a night! The dance, and the dance-off, and winning the prize, and the kidnapping, and the shoot-out . . .

Then Tommy was standing over him. "Turn it off," he said quietly. "Turn off the TV and be quiet."

"Are we going to bed?"

"Turn it off," Tommy whispered. "That guy's in your backyard again."

Tommy got down on his hands and knees and crawled across the floor to the window. Nicky followed.

Outside, moving through the shadows behind the pool house, was the man the boys had seen sneaking around the day before the Snow Ball. He was bundled up in a black parka, a black ski hat and a muffler, and he was fifty feet away, but there was no question that it was the same man. Was it the same man they had seen with Nicky's mother at the mall? Nicky couldn't be sure. But it was almost definitely the man he had seen her with at the party.

"What does he want?" Nicky whispered.

"Who knows?" Tommy said. "But it ain't good."

"Should we wake up my uncle?"

"I don't know," Tommy said. "But we gotta do *something*. Who knows what he's planning to do?"

The boys stared. The man in the yard once again appeared to be sizing up the house. He walked from behind the pool house to the center of the yard, behind some pine trees. Then he crouched down and stared at the house some more.

"He's like a sniper or something," Tommy said.

"*Shhh,*" Nicky said. "He's looking right at us."

"Where's he going?"

The man walked directly across the backyard then, passing the pool and going around the side of the house. Nicky and Tommy crouched, afraid to move. They heard a car door open and close. Amy's Dobermans started to growl and snarl.

The car didn't start. Instead, the man again walked across the backyard. He was carrying a black satchel over his shoulder. He went back down near the trees and unzipped the satchel. He took out a black metal tripod, which he set up facing the house. Nicky could hear Amy's Dobermans barking and growling.

"Check it out!" Tommy said. "He's a pro. He's got a tripod!"

"I bet he works for Van Allen," Nicky said. "He probably knows we set him up. What are we gonna *do*?"

"I don't know," Tommy said. "But we gotta do something. Man! He's lining up his shots with a laser!" Tommy said. "Whatever we're gonna do, we gotta do it *fast*."

"The dogs," Nicky said. "Amy's dogs."

"I hear them. So what?"

"That's the plan!"

"What is?"

"We'll go down and open the gate," Nicky said. "Those guys'll come tearing in and chase him off."

"Okay," Tommy said, "but if you open the gate, won't they bite you?"

"No," Nicky said. "They know me. But wait. That's no good. He'll just shoot the dogs. I don't want him to shoot the dogs."

"Better he should shoot the dogs than shoot your dad!" Tommy said. "Or us!"

"Yes, but . . ." Nicky thought. "What about this? I'll sneak around to the bottom of the yard. You go over to the gate and turn the dogs loose. They'll go flying toward him. While he's distracted, I'll grab his gun and run away with it."

"That's a terrible plan," Tommy said. "There's no way I'm going to turn the dogs loose, first of all. And he'll get to the gun before you do, second of all."

"Do you have a better plan?"

The man focused the laser and sighted along it toward the house.

"No," Tommy said. "I don't."

"All right," Nicky whispered. "Here's the deal. You open the gate. I'll call the dogs. As soon as they come through the gate, you go through it the other way—into Amy's yard—and shut it behind you. The dogs will see him and go crazy. He'll freak out and start running. Or shooting. The dogs will get him. I'll get his gun. We'll hold him until the police come."

"This is never going to work," Tommy said.

"I know," Nicky said. "Put your boots on."

The sun was coming up over Carrington. The eastern sky was pink. The tops of the trees were lighted. Nicky and Tommy went to the front door and crept quietly around the side of the house. They walked across Nicky's yard and across the frozen stream leading to Amy's house. Behind the fence, the dogs growled until they recognized Nicky.

"Good boys," Nicky said. "Good doggies. Wait until I wave to let them out, okay?"

The dogs started growling again. Tommy said, "I'm a dead man." But Nicky was already gone.

Nicky moved along the bottom of the yard, circling behind the pool house and through the trees. His feet made quiet crunching sounds in the snow. A bird called and startled him. Over his shoulder, he could see Tommy crouching by the gate. Ahead of him, he could see the stranger staring at the house through his scope and bending down to take something else out of his bag.

It was time. Nicky got to his knees and waved to Tommy. The gate flew open.

Nicky called, "Prince! Duke! Get 'im!"

Then he heard the gate slam.

The dogs went across the yard like growling thunder. The stranger heard them first, then looked up and saw

189

them. He froze. Then he panicked. He spun around, looking for a way out. There wasn't one. He began to run for the front of the house. Then he turned and ran back toward the pool house. Nicky saw that he would never make it. The dogs were running too fast.

The man must have seen that, too. The dogs were almost on him. He screamed. Then he leapt into the swimming pool.

There was a great splash. The dogs jerked to a halt, and a wave of water crested over them. They shook themselves and stood staring into the pool.

"The gun!" Tommy shouted. "Nicky! Get his gun!"

Nicky had forgotten. He ran to the man's tripod and yanked open the satchel. He found a level, and a notebook, and a T square. He looked through the scope trained on the house, but he couldn't see anything.

By now the man had sputtered to the surface. He looked at the dogs, who growled at him. The man began to splash around. He reached for the side of the pool, but the growling dogs pushed him back.

So he shouted for help.

Lights went on inside Nicky's house. Nicky heard pounding feet, then a door slammed open. His father burst into the backyard in his pajamas, followed shortly by Nicky's uncle Frankie—running from Marian Galloway's house! He pushed past Tommy and ran through the gate.

"Nicky!" he called.

"He's by the pool!" Tommy shouted. "He's okay."

"Dad!" Nicky shouted. "Look! We trapped the sniper!"

"You what?"

"The sniper! We caught him! He was getting ready to shoot, and me and Tommy stopped him!"

Nicky's father skidded to a halt. He stared at the splashing man in the pool, and at his son, and at the Dobermans.

"Nice work, Nicholas," he said. "Some sniper. You've actually trapped the contractor. Good morning, Dennis. I'm—I'm sorry. Swim over to the side here. I'll help you out. Nicky, put those dogs away."

"It was supposed to be a surprise," Nicky's mother said a half hour later. "Dennis was going to build you an art studio. For the backyard. For you to work in. It was *supposed* to be for your birthday."

The family were in the breakfast room—Nicky's mom and dad, and Uncle Frankie, and Grandma Tutti, who was busy making coffee. Nicky and Tommy were still in their pajamas. Donna, wearing one of Nicky's mother's bathrobes, was holding a mug of tea. For the moment, everyone was staring at Nicky.

He hung his head.

"What were you thinking?" his father said. "Was this Tommy's idea?"

"No," Nicky said. "It was all my idea. Because, see, I had already seen this guy prowling around the backyard. And then I saw him at the mall with Mom. And at the Snow Ball. And then he showed up here, and it was barely even light out, and he was carrying this gun bag, and he set up a tripod, and he had this laser thing like he was taking aim at the *house*."

"And from that you imagined that he was a trained assassin?" his father said. "Sent here to *kill* me?"

"I know it sounds ridiculous," Nicky said. "But after the whole thing with Patrick Arlen, and Peter Van Allen . . ."

"But the police had them—I mean him—already."

"I didn't know what to think," Nicky said.

"So you concocted a plan to have him attacked by the next-door neighbors' Dobermans?"

"Well, it wasn't much of a plan," Nicky said. "But he was in the backyard! Practically in the middle of the night! With a laser gun!"

"It's called a level," his father said. "It was part of Dennis' surveying equipment. For the art studio."

"He was here to see the morning light, to see where it would be best for a painter," his mother said. "A painter *must* have good northern exposure. It was going to be a beautiful studio! We were at Silver Art Supply looking at pictures of *gazebos*."

Tommy leaned over to Nicky and whispered, "What's a gazebo?"

"Not now, Tommy," Nicky said.

"Well, so much for that," Nicky's father said. "You saw the look on his face. I don't imagine he'll be coming back to build the studio, anyway."

"Aw, come on!" Uncle Frankie said. "It was an honest mistake. You want me to talk to him for you?"

"No!" Nicky's father and mother said at the same time.

192

"I'll make him an offer," Nicky's father said. "That is, if you still think you want an art studio for your birthday."

"Yes!" Nicky said. "I think it's a great birthday present."

"You're lucky you're getting anything, you hoodlum," Uncle Frankie said. "And you, Tommy! That was amazing with the GPS thing and all, but do you guys get into trouble every time you're together? I oughta—"

"Stop!" Grandma Tutti said. "Nicky was trying to protect his family. And Tommy was trying to help. He's a good boy! You should all stop picking on both of them!"

"I agree," Frankie said.

"I disagree," Nicky's father said. "But we'll drop it, for now."

"Good!" Grandma Tutti said. "It's breakfast time, anyway. If Donna and Tommy and Nicky would give me some help, I'll make *zeppoli*."

"All right!" Nicky said, and jumped toward the kitchen.

"Wait!" Nicky's father said to him. "Say you're sorry and hug your mother. *Then* we can all have some breakfast."

"And *zeppoli*!" Nicky said. He threw himself into his mother's arms and then went to help Grandma Tutti make his favorite so the family could enjoy it together.

Grandma Tutti's Pasta e Fagioli
(Noodles and Beans)
aka Pasta Fazool

This is the most comforting of all Italian comfort foods—sort of like Italian chicken soup for the soul. It's easy to make and it's very satisfying. Some Italian families serve it by itself for a meal. Other families eat it for starters, then tuck into the real meal. Either way, it's a delicious, healthy bowl of soup. Here are two recipes. One is Grandma Tutti's. The other is Nicky's mom's. Not for nothing, but we prefer Grandma Tutti's.

SERVES 4

- 1/2 pound dry cannellini beans or great northern beans
    or
- 1 8-ounce can cannellini beans, drained
- 1/2 teaspoon salt
- 1 bay leaf
- 1 tablespoon olive oil
- 1/2 pound beef stew meat, cut into 1/2-inch pieces
- 2 cloves garlic, peeled
- 1 teaspoon sweet basil
- 1 28-ounce can whole tomatoes
- 1/2 pound pasta—any kind, but macaroni is best

If you're using dry beans, put them in a soup pot, salt them and cover them with water the night before. Then add the bay leaf, bring to a boil and simmer until the beans are soft, about one hour, always keeping the beans covered with water.

If you're using canned beans, continue.

Heat the olive oil in a deep, wide saucepan. Brown the meat over a medium flame for about five minutes. Add the cloves of garlic and the basil. Pour the tomatoes, with their juices, into a blender or a food processor. Add one cup of the cooked or canned beans. (Discard the bay leaf.) Pulse for 15 seconds. Add the tomato/bean mixture, and the beans you didn't put in the blender, to the saucepan.

Heat water in a pot until boiling. Add the macaroni and cook until it's soft—11 to 13 minutes. Then add all the noodles to the saucepan, along with enough of the macaroni water to make your soup the right consistency. Serve with grated Parmesan cheese and a nice Italian bread.

For Nicky D.'s mom's version, leave out the meat. It's vegetarian pasta fazool!

STEVEN R. SCHIRRIPA is best known to television audiences as Bobby "Bacala" Baccalieri on the HBO hit series *The Sopranos*. He has also become a regular field correspondent for *The Tonight Show with Jay Leno* and appeared as host for Spike TV's *Casino Cinema* series. Steve is developing a half-hour situation comedy based on his bestselling book *A Goomba's Guide to Life*, coauthored, along with *The Goomba's Book of Love* and *The Goomba Diet*, with Charles Fleming. Steve lives with his wife and their two daughters in New York City and Las Vegas.

CHARLES FLEMING is the coauthor of the 2003 *New York Times* bestseller *Three Weeks in October: The Manhunt for the Serial Sniper*. He is the author of the 1998 *Los Angeles Times* bestseller *High Concept: Don Simpson and the Hollywood Culture of Excess* and the novels *The Ivory Coast* and *After Havana*. He is a veteran entertainment reporter and columnist for such publications as *Newsweek*, *Variety*, and *Vanity Fair* and an adjunct professor of journalism at the University of Southern California's Annenberg School for Communication. He lives with his wife and their two daughters in Los Angeles.